The Mystery at Claudia's House
Ann M. Martin

AN
APPLE
PAPERBACK

SCHOLASTIC INC.
New York Toronto London Auckland Sydney

Cover art by Hodges Soileau

ISBN 0-590-44961-3

12 11 10 9 8 7 6 5 4 3 2 1   2 3 4 5 6 7/9

Printed in the U.S.A.   28

First Scholastic printing, November 1992

The Mystery at Claudia's House

**Other books by
Ann M. Martin**

Ma and Pa Dracula
Yours Turly, Shirley
Ten Kids, No Pets
Slam Book
Just a Summer Romance
Missing Since Monday
With You and Without You
Me and Katie (the Pest)
Stage Fright
Inside Out
Bummer Summer

The author gratefully acknowledges
Ellen Miles
for her help in
preparing this manuscript.

The Mystery at Claudia's House

CHAPTER 1

"Oh, Lamont, you shouldn't have!" squealed Becca. "These flowers are *so* gorgeous. But I don't know where I can possibly fit them! My entire house is already *full* of the beautiful flowers you've brought me."

"Well, actually," said Charlotte, putting on a deep voice, "these aren't for you. They're for Charlotte, and they're from Derek!"

Charlotte and Becca broke into hysterical giggles. Charlotte stuck the bouquet of flowers (actually a crumpled sheet of newspaper) behind a chair and turned to me. "Isn't it awesome? Derek Masters is coming back to town!"

"It's great," I agreed, hiding a smile. And to tell the truth, it *was* kind of exciting. Not every little town has a real live TV star. I could understand why the girls were so wild about the news.

"The girls" were Charlotte Johanssen and Becca Ramsey. I was baby-sitting for Charlotte,

1

and Becca, who is Charlotte's best friend, was visiting. Who am I? I'm Claudia Kishi. I'm thirteen years old and I'm in eighth grade at Stoneybrook Middle School. Stoneybrook, Connecticut, that is. That's the name of the town I live in. And the town Derek Masters would soon be returning to!

Derek Masters, in case you're wondering, is an actual, genuine TV star. He's on this really popular show called *P.S. 162*, about a class in an inner-city elementary school. The character he plays is called Waldo, and he (the character, not Derek) is kind of a geek. But he's a *funny* geek, and the other kids in the class like him. He's not the most popular kid, though. That would be Lamont, who's smart, and funny, and really cute. Lamont is the one Becca has a giant crush on.

Anyway, Derek Masters lived in Stoneybrook long ago before he even *dreamed* of becoming a star. He used to do a little modeling and stuff like that, and then he was discovered and hit the big time. So now he lives out in L.A. most of the time, since that's where his work is. But whenever he has a chunk of time off, he and his family come back to Stoneybrook, where they still have a house.

"How long is Derek staying this time?" I asked Charlotte. She seemed to have all the inside information on Derek and his plans.

"Well, his show's on hiatus," she said knowingly. "So I guess he'll be here for a couple of months."

"His show is on *what*?" I said.

"On hiatus. It's just a break," said Becca. "Like, they've already made all the shows for this season, so now they have some time off until they start again."

"How do you know so much about this stuff?" I asked. I was amazed at how sophisticated they sounded, for eight-year-olds.

"Derek told Nicky all about it," said Charlotte. "And Nicky told us."

Nicky is Nicky Pike, who is Derek's best friend in Stoneybrook. "So, did Nicky tell you when Derek will be here?" I asked.

"Today!" cried Charlotte. "He's coming today!" She sounded like an eight-year-old again.

"But we probably won't see him for a few days," added Becca. "He might not start school until Monday."

"I don't know if I can *stand* it," said Charlotte, dramatically. "It's only Wednesday. How can I wait five whole days to see him?"

"Well, you've already waited for about five *months*," pointed out Becca. "I think you'll make it." She sounded very mature. Then she started to giggle. "But I don't know if *I* will! I can't *wait* to see him. Maybe this time he got Lamont's autograph for me!"

The girls started to talk excitedly about what they would wear to school on Monday, and what they would say to Derek when they saw him. I listened for a bit, and then I tuned out. Poor Derek. When he's in Stoneybrook, what he wants most of all is to be treated like a regular kid, not like a star. He likes to do all the things other eight-year-old boys do. He's a good big brother to his little brother, Todd. And, while he sometimes has trouble re-adjusting to "normal" life, he's basically just a smart, friendly guy. I hoped the other kids would give him room to be himself, instead of treating him like someone famous. I can understand why he hates that.

I understand a lot about kids. I kind of pride myself on that. It's not necessarily because I have a natural talent for it, though — it's just because I'm around kids a lot. I baby-sit all the time, and it's something I love to do. In fact, I'm in this club — the Baby-sitters Club or BSC. It's a group of girls — and one boy — who love to baby-sit and who have gotten together and made kind of a business of it. I'll explain more about the club later.

Understanding kids may not be one of my *natural* talents, but I do have some of those. Mainly what I'm talented at is art. I love all kinds of art, and without being egotistical about it, I have to say I'm a pretty good artist.

Not that I love everything I do. I've drawn plenty of pictures only to rip them up, and started and never finished a bunch of sculptures. But I've also done some things I'm proud of, and things other people seem to like a lot.

I'm always working on some project. Sometimes it's handmade jewelry, which I love to wear or give as gifts. Sometimes it's a sculpture or a collage. Other times it's a series of paintings, like the ones I did of junk food. Yes, junk food. That's one of my other loves. I could eat Twinkies and Doritos all day long. I think my paintings really showed how much I love the stuff, too, because the objects in the paintings — a Chunky bar, a pack of Lifesavers—look *beautiful*. They're kind of like portraits. Portraits of loved ones.

Pretty silly, right? Oh well, maybe you have to see them to understand. Anyway, I do love art. And junk food. What else? Well, I love to read mysteries — especially Nancy Drew stories. My parents don't approve because they think those books'll rot my brain. (They don't approve of junk food, because they think it'll rot my teeth!) But I keep on reading — and eating — what I like. I just keep the books and food hidden, and figure what my parents don't know won't hurt them.

Except for their lack of taste in food and

reading material, my parents are basically great people. They are Japanese-American like me. And although they can be strict, they are also fair. They do their best to treat me and my older sister equally, even though sometimes I think Janine (that's my sister) gets more attention than I do. The fact is, she earns attention by doing exceptional things, like getting all A pluses, for example, or by being invited to join this program in which she attends college classes even though she's still in high school.

Janine's a genius. I mean it. She's not just smart or intelligent. She's a *super-brain*. Sometimes I wonder how we're even in the same family. I mean, I'm not dumb, but I don't do well in school. I never have, and I probably never will. And you know what? I don't really care. I mean, sure I wish I were a better student, but being a good artist means more to me. I know my parents think I should "apply" myself, since my teachers say that that's all I need to do to get better grades. But I guess things like spelling and math just aren't that important to me.

Janine sometimes teases me and tells me I'm "shallow" because I'm interested in hairstyles and cool clothes. I'll admit that I love to wear trendy stuff — in fact, sometimes I'm even the one to *invent* trends in my school. And I do love to try all kinds of wild things with my hair, which is long and black and straight. I even love to experiment with makeup. I like to try accentuating certain features. But I don't think that makes me shallow. These things are part of my artistic nature. I see my body as a blank canvas, and I can put anything I want onto that canvas, depending on my mood. Does that make any sense?

I was thinking this over, and checking that day's outfit (lace leggings, purple tie-dyed T-shirt dress, and purple high-tops) in the mirror, when I was snapped back to reality by Charlotte who was tugging on my sleeve.

"Becca and I want to make 'welcome back' cards for Derek. Can you help us?"

"Sure," I said. "That sounds like fun." I love working on art projects with kids. "Let's put down some newspaper, and then we can take out the poster paints and get crazy!"

Pretty soon we were sprawled out on the floor, making a big mess. (I had decided to make a card too, just for fun.) Charlotte covered her paintbrush with drippy red paint. "Derek's going to love this card," she said. "I'm making a picture of him as Waldo. You know, with those funny glasses and that spiky hair?"

Derek-in-person looks so different from Derek-as-Waldo. The first time I met him I could hardly believe Derek really was the same person I'd seen on TV. In real life he's totally normal-looking, but on the show he gets laughs just by walking into the room.

"I like Waldo," mused Becca. "He's funny. But Lamont! Lamont is really special. He is *so* cute. Did you ever notice how big his eyes are?" I think one of the reasons Becca picked Lamont to have a crush on is because he's African-American. Becca is, too. And she doesn't have too many black friends in Stoneybrook, because not that many black people live here. She used to live in New Jersey, in a more integrated town. Anyway, she probably likes Lamont because she relates to him and wishes she knew more boys like him.

It must be hard sometimes for Becca and her family. I'm friends with her older sister Jessi (she's in the BSC), and I know that when they first moved here people were actually mean to them. By now they've been accepted, but it wasn't easy at first.

Charlotte and Becca and I spent the rest of the afternoon finishing our cards and talking about Derek and his show. Just as we were cleaning up, Dr. Johanssen, Charlotte's mom, came home. It was already five o'clock by then, so I said my good-byes and headed back to my house to get ready for our club meeting, which is always at five-thirty and always in my room.

The house was quiet. I knew my parents were still at work. I also knew where I could find Janine. She was, as usual, in her room. Studying. What else is new? I stopped in to say hi to her, and then went into my own room, thinking I should tidy it up a little before the meeting.

As soon as I walked in, I noticed something strange. My room was messy, but that wasn't the strange thing. It's always messy. The strange thing was the *way* it was messy. It was different. Somebody *else* had made it messy, not me. On my desk, my papers were disorganized in an unfamiliar way. The makeup on my dresser was spread out differently than it had been that morning. And my closet door was hanging open even though I knew that, for once, I'd left it shut that morning.

I couldn't believe it! Had my room been burglarized, even though the rest of the house looked like it hadn't been touched? I started to panic. Then I looked carefully around the room and began to calm down. Nothing was missing. I could see that right away.

At that moment, my friends Kristy and Mary Anne arrived. I wasn't going to have time to put my room back in order because it was almost five-thirty and our club meeting was about to start.

CHAPTER 2

"Can you believe this?" I said, gesturing at the mess on my desk and dresser.

"What?" asked Kristy.

"My *room*," I said.

"What about it?" asked Mary Anne. "It looks the same as always."

I had to laugh. "I guess it does. But this is a *different* kind of mess than usual. Someone was in here!"

"You're kidding!" said Kristy. "What did they take?"

"Nothing that I know of," I admitted. "But still — "

"Tell us about it after the meeting," interrupted Kristy. The other members of the club had arrived by then, and my digital clock had turned to five-thirty. Kristy is very punctual and always starts our meetings on time. She's also very focused, and never lets anything get in the way of club business.

Even though Kristy can drive me nuts sometimes, I'm glad she's our club president. If she weren't, I don't know if we'd ever get anything done. The rest of us would be happy to discuss school or the latest issue of *People* magazine for hours at a time, but Kristy keeps us focused on the club.

But that's not the only reason she's president. The main reason is that she thought up the idea for the club. Kristy's always having great ideas, and this was the most awesome. She figured parents would think it was convenient to be able to call one phone number and reach a bunch of good sitters — and she was right. Business has been booming since the day the club started. Here's how it works: we meet every Monday, Wednesday, and Friday from five-thirty to six. We advertised those hours at first, with fliers, but we hardly ever have to do that anymore. Parents call to line up sitters, and we divide up the jobs according to who's available when. Simple, right? But it took Kristy Thomas to think of it.

Kristy's a real dynamo. She has brown hair and brown eyes, and she's short for her age. She's kind of a tomboy: Kristy loves sports, especially baseball. And she doesn't care much about clothes and makeup and all that. She wears nearly the same thing every day: jeans, a turtleneck, and running shoes.

Kristy has a big family, and it's much more complicated than mine. She has two older brothers and one younger one, plus a stepfather and *his* kids — a boy and a girl — from his first marriage. (Her stepbrother and stepsister don't live with Kristy all the time, though. Most of the time they're with their mom.) Also, her mom and stepdad adopted a little girl, so Kristy has a two-year-old sister, too. Plus, her grandmother lives with the family. It's a full house, but luckily Kristy's stepdad (whose name is Watson Brewer) is a millionaire — honest! — and their house is actually a mansion.

That's Kristy. Now, more about the club she organized. I'm the vice-president. Why? Well, mainly because we meet in my room and use my private phone line for our business. I guess I don't have any real duties, unless you count supplying Ring-Dings and Ruffles. Oh, and I also take care of any business calls that come in during times when we're *not* meeting.

Mary Anne Spier is our secretary. She's Kristy's best friend, even though they are very different people. I think the only thing they have in common may be their looks: Mary Anne also has brown hair and eyes, and is small for her age. But while Kristy is outgoing, Mary Anne is more of a mouse. She's shy, and quiet, and very sensitive.

Everybody loves Mary Anne, because she's a good listener and a good friend. She's not very sophisticated, but in a way she's more mature than she seems. For example, she's the only one in the club who has a steady boyfriend! Also, she's very dependable, which is important for the club. As secretary, she takes care of a lot of little details. She keeps our record book up-to-date with all kinds of information about our clients. She also keeps track of everyone's schedule, so when a call comes in she always knows — at a glance — who's available.

Mary Anne's mom died a long, long time ago, and Mary Anne grew up with just her father. I know life wasn't always easy for Mary Anne *or* her father. But now Mary Anne has a new stepmom, *and* a new stepsister and -brother. More about that later.

Our club's treasurer is Stacey McGill, who happens to be my best friend. Stacey is cool. Very cool. She grew up in New York City, and I think she's more sophisticated than anyone else in Stoneybrook. Her outfits are always awesome, and she perms her blonde hair and wears makeup that brings out her big blue eyes.

Stacey's parents got divorced not too long ago, and her dad lives in New York. Stacey visits him as often as she can, but I think she's

13

glad she decided to live in Stoneybrook with her mom. (Boy, would I hate to have had to make that kind of decision!) I think Stacey has a really good relationship with her mother. Mrs. McGill used to baby Stacey, because Stacey has diabetes. But by now Stacey has proved that she is mature enough to take care of herself.

Diabetes is no joke. It's a serious disease, and Stacey will always have it. It has to do with blood sugar; I've never entirely understood the scientific explanation, but I know that Stacey has to be very careful about what she eats. No sweets. (That would be a total nightmare for me.) Also, she has to give herself a shot every single day. That's because her body doesn't produce the right amount of this stuff which I forget the name of. Anyway, Stacey's very accepting about having diabetes, even though it sometimes makes her really, really sick.

As treasurer of our club, Stacey's main job is to collect dues every Monday. She sometimes has to pry the money out of us, since we all *hate* to part with our hard-earned cash. She also keeps track of how much money is in the treasury. This is a snap for Stacey. She loves math. (Gag me!)

We use the dues money for a lot of different things. For example, we pay Kristy's brother to drive her to meetings, since Watson's mansion is way across town. (Kristy used to live across the street from me.) And some of the money goes for supplies for our Kid-Kits. Kid-Kits are another of Kristy's great ideas. They're these boxes we've decorated to look cool, and they're full of stuff that kids love: games and puzzles and stickers and books. We bring them on jobs, and they're always a big hit, especially on rainy days when kids are bored to death with all their *own* toys.

If Stacey can't make a meeting some day, Dawn Schafer can take over her job. In fact, Dawn can take over any job in the club. She's our alternate officer, and she can fill in for anyone. Dawn's great. She's also absolutely gorgeous, but she doesn't even know it. She has this long, long silky blonde hair, and big blue eyes, and this great casual-yet-extremely-stylish way of dressing.

Dawn and her younger brother grew up in California, but when her parents got divorced, her mom decided to move back to Stoneybrook, which was where *she'd* grown up. Guess what happened to Mrs. Schafer when she came back to Stoneybrook? She met this man she used to date in high school, fell in love with him again, and married him. And guess who that man was? Incredible but true: It was Mary Anne's father. That's how Mary

Anne acquired a new stepmother and stepsister and stepbrother.

Dawn still misses California sometimes, but now she loves Stoneybrook and considers it her home. Her brother never made that adjustment, though. He went back to California to live with his dad. I know that's hard on Dawn. She misses Jeff a lot.

Kristy and Mary Anne and Stacey and Dawn and I are all thirteen and in the eighth grade, but two members of our club are a little younger. They are our junior officers, Mallory Pike and Jessi Ramsey, who are eleven and in the sixth grade. They're also best friends. Being junior officers means that they can't baby-sit on weeknights, unless it's for their own families. Instead, they do a lot of afternoon sitting, which is great since it frees the rest of us up for nights.

Mallory is energetic and smart. She has red hair and wears glasses. She also has braces, which she hates. Mal would love to have her braces removed, dump her glasses for contacts, and get some really funky clothes to wear — but she *is* only eleven, and her parents have told her she'll just have to wait. I think Mal sometimes feels older than her years, because she's the eldest in a family of eight kids and has had a lot of responsibility for her brothers and sisters. Mal wants to write and illustrate children's books someday, and I think she'll probably do just that. She has a lot of talent.

I've already told you a little about Jessi. Becca is her sister, remember? She also has a baby brother, who is adorable. Like Mal, Jessi is talented; she's a dancer. She's been studying ballet forever, and she's really serious about it. Her parents are totally supportive of her, which is great. Jessi's family also includes an aunt who lives with them.

There are two more members of our club, but they don't come to meetings. They're associate members, who help out when our schedule is overloaded. One is Shannon Kilbourne, a girl from Kristy's neighborhood. The other is Logan Bruno, who happens to be Mary Anne's boyfriend.

So that's the club. Great idea, great people. There's only one tiny little thing about our club that I don't love. That's the club notebook, another of Kristy's ideas, in which we each have to write up what happens on every job we go on. Then we all read the notebook every week, so we're up to date on what's going on with our clients. Good idea, right? So why don't I like it? Well, since I don't happen to be the world's best speller, sometimes I get a little embarrassed about how my entries look. But I write in the book anyway, because it *is* a good idea. Besides, Kristy insists on it.

Our meeting that day was almost over. In between phone calls and after we'd taken care of club business, I told everyone about how I thought someone had been in my room. Nobody took this seriously; maybe they didn't believe me. After all, my room didn't look all that different to *them*. Jessi jokingly suggested that the FBI must be after me for some reason, and Dawn thought maybe it was the work of a ghost. (She *loves* ghost stories.) Kristy wanted me to set up an elaborate trap to catch whoever *might* have been in my room, but the others didn't think it was worth the work. I decided they were right. In fact, I decided the whole thing probably *had* been in my head.

Just as the meeting was ending, guess who called. Derek Masters' mom! So he *was* back in town. Mrs. Masters said she'd be needing sitters quite often, since she and Mr. Masters were very busy managing Derek's career. I have to admit that we squabbled just a little over who would get the first job — everybody was kind of excited about sitting for a STAR — but Kristy was actually the only one free that Friday, which was the day Mrs. Masters was calling about. So she got the job.

After the meeting, I put my room back in

order, checking again to make sure nothing was missing. Nothing was. I figured I had just imagined the whole thing. After all, why would anyone be interested in my makeup and stuff? It didn't make sense.

CHAPTER 3

Friday

It sure was great to see Derek again. I'll admit that it took me a little while to remember that he's a kid first and a TV star second — but once I got over that part, we had a good time together. You know what else? Todd is a great kid, too. He's lots of fun, and he doesn't seem to mind that his big brother gets so much attention. Of course, he may be just a tiny bit resentful at times; that's probably why he spilled the beans about Derek's Big Secret.

Kristy was a little nervous about being the first to sit for the Masters boys. She hadn't seen Derek for a long time. For all she knew, he might have changed a lot.

"What if he thinks of himself as a big star now?" she'd asked Mary Anne and me at lunch. "After all, his show's more popular than ever now. Maybe he won't even talk to normal people anymore. He probably has a car phone and a swimming pool and all kinds of things out there in Hollywood. He's going to be so bored in Stoneybrook. How'm I supposed to entertain a kid like that? He's probably ten times more sophisticated than I'll *ever* be." Kristy sounded so panicked that I was tempted to giggle. I was sitting next to her in the school cafeteria, Mary Anne was across the table, and Stacey, Dawn, and Logan were scattered around us.

"Kristy," said Mary Anne. "You're getting carried away. He's only a kid, remember? I'm sure he hasn't changed at all. He was really friendly to Jessi, that time she visited him when we were all out in California. Anyway, you can handle him, whatever he's like. You're a great baby-sitter."

Good old Mary Anne. She always knows just what to say. There I was, ready to laugh at Kristy's fears, but Mary Anne kept a straight face and calmed Kristy right down. I'll never be as sensitive as Mary Anne.

"Mary Anne's right," I said. "Just treat him like a regular kid, and you'll be fine." Then I remembered something and started to laugh. "Did you see the show last night? The one where Waldo gets new glasses and starts to think he has X-ray vision? It was *so* funny."

Mary Anne giggled. "Dawn and I were watching," she said. "We were both practically *dying* from laughing so hard."

Kristy just looked at us. "See what I mean?" she said. "He's a big star. Everybody talks about that show *all day* after it's on." She shook her head and took another bite of her peanut-butter-and-jelly sandwich. Kristy hadn't said one word about what my friends and I were eating, which was very unusual. Normally she would have spent the whole lunch period teasing about how gross the chicken chow mein looked. Instead, she just talked about how worried she was. It was unlike Kristy to be so nervous about a sitting job, but I guess anybody can get starstruck.

Kristy spent that whole day worrying about her job at the Masterses'. I noticed during our meeting that afternoon that she seemed distracted, and later I found out why.

"I was trying to figure out what I should wear," said Kristy. "It seemed like I should dress up a little, since Derek is so famous." I was shocked. Kristy *never* dresses up. But that night she changed out of her jeans and into freshly ironed dress pants, just for Derek.

By the time Kristy knocked on the Masterses' door, she had butterflies in her stomach. Mrs. Masters answered the door. She was flustered because she and Mr. Masters had a big meeting planned with Derek's agent. They ran out with hardly a word to Kristy. But just as the door slammed behind them, Derek appeared in the hall and a funny thing happened. The second Kristy saw him, her nervousness melted away. For one thing, she'd forgotten that Derek looks nothing like the character he plays on TV. He doesn't wear glasses, or have a spiky haircut. He's just a normal, friendly looking kid. And for another thing, he looked awfully glad to see Kristy. "Derek!" she said. "How *are* you?"

"I'm great," he said, smiling. "I'm so happy to be back in Stoneybrook. I get *bored* in Hollywood."

Kristy stifled a giggle. "I thought your life out there was glamorous and exciting," she said.

"Not really," he answered. "I work hard, you know. And then, I get tutored on the set with the other kids from the show. Sometimes I just really miss being with regular kids at a normal school!"

"I'll bet," said Kristy. "Well, I'm sure your old Stoneybrook friends are happy to see you." Kristy was glad she could say that — and *mean* it. She knew it was true. But Derek hadn't always been so popular in Stoneybrook. When he first became famous, he'd had a hard time in school for quite a while. Jessi had been his main baby-sitter at the time, and she was amazed at how mean to him the other kids were. According to Derek, they teased him and picked fights with him all the time. The meanest kid was one named John. After hearing all the stories about what John did, Jessi nicknamed him "Superbrat." But you know what? John didn't really exist. And all those mean things he had supposedly done were actually done by — get this — *Derek*! He was just having a hard time adjusting to being a star. He wasn't sure anymore how a "normal" kid was supposed to act. But Derek got through that phase with a little help from Jessi. And Kristy knew that, this time around, the kids at Stoneybrook Elementary were thrilled to have him back at school.

Derek started to tell Kristy about the teepee his class was building, but just then Todd, who's four, came running into the room.

"Hi!" he said, stopping short when he saw Kristy. "Who are you?"

Kristy laughed. "I'm Kristy," she said. "I

used to baby-sit for you, but I guess you don't remember. Anyway, I'm here to watch you and Derek."

"Oh, okay," said Todd. He gave Kristy a big smile. "Want to come see what I made with my Legos?"

"Sure," said Kristy. She and Derek followed Todd into the living room. "Hey, that's great," she said, when she saw what Todd had made. It was a big castle, with towers and everything.

"My dad helped," admitted Todd. "So did Derek." He squatted down and started to take apart the drawbridge.

Kristy and Derek sat on the couch to watch him. "Your show was great last night," said Kristy shyly. "You were really funny."

"Thanks," said Derek. "I have fun doing that show, but sometimes I get a little tired of playing Waldo. He's such a geek!"

Kristy laughed.

"Did you see me on *Kid Detectives* last month?" asked Derek. "That show is awesome. It was so great to work on something different."

"You were on *Kid Detectives*?" asked Kristy. "I *love* that show. But I didn't see it when you were on." *Kid Detectives* is this show on which a real-life mystery is acted out, and then solved by, like, the victim's little brother or his best friend. It's not usually about murders or scary stuff like that; it's more likely to be about a stolen skateboard or something. We all love the show.

"I was on a couple of times," said Derek. "I learned a lot about crime-solving, too. I'm an expert now."

"Cool," said Kristy. "Boy, it sounds like you've been busy. Going to school and doing homework every night is going to seem like a vacation, right?"

"Well, I wouldn't go that far," said Derek, laughing. "You should see the book I have to read by next week!"

"Do you have a lot of catching up to do?" asked Kristy.

"Yeah, but Nicky Pike is going to help me," said Derek. "So are some of the other kids."

"Great," said Kristy. "So, no problems with any kids at school this time?"

"Nope," said Derek. "Well, except for one thing."

"What?" asked Kristy.

"They all keep bugging me to tell them what's going to happen next season on *P.S. 162*."

Kristy laughed. "I can understand why they're curious. I'm dying to know, myself. I mean, I heard a rumor that Lamont is going to quit the show. Is that true? That would be a shame."

26

"No, no," said Derek. "He's staying."

"Oh," said Kristy. "So what are the kids at school asking about?"

"Nothing," said Derek, turning away. "Just forget it."

Kristy raised her eyebrows. Derek was acting awfully sensitive all of a sudden. Then she heard a funny noise. She looked over at Todd, who was still working on his castle. Todd was making kissing noises, and grinning at Derek. Kristy looked back at Derek. He had turned bright red.

"Cut that out!" he yelled at Todd.

"Oh, my darling," said Todd, in a high voice. "Kiss me again!" He puckered up his lips.

"Todd!" said Derek. He looked angry.

Kristy was bewildered. "What's going on?" she asked.

"Ask Derek," said Todd, knowingly. "Or . . . his girlfriend."

"She's not my girlfriend!" cried Derek. He was still blushing. "She's just an actress."

"Ohhh," said Kristy, beginning to understand. "I think I get it. Is Waldo going to have a crush on Jennifer?" Jennifer is this character on the show. She's good friends with Waldo. The girl who plays Jennifer is super-gorgeous, by the way. She has long black hair and blue eyes, which is an unusual combination.

Derek folded his arms in front of his chest and didn't answer. Kristy looked at Todd, who gave her a big grin and nodded. "Well, I think that's sweet, Derek," said Kristy. "I like Jennifer, and she and Waldo have been good friends for a long time. Why *shouldn't* they have a little romance?"

"I don't care if they do," said Derek. "But why does he have to — ugh!"

Todd made the kissing noise again.

"*Kiss* her?" asked Kristy. "You're going to kiss Jennifer on the show?"

"*I'm* not," said Derek. "*Waldo* is. And it's supposed to be a secret. If you tell anybody — "

"Right," said Kristy. Obviously, Derek had a big problem with the idea of kissing a girl, so she decided to change the subject before he became too upset. "Hey, listen," she said. "Weren't you going to tell me about that teepee you're building?"

"Yeah!" he said, sounding relieved. "Wait here. I'll go get the book we're reading. It's all about Native Americans."

Kristy breathed a sigh of relief as Derek ran upstairs. She told Todd to stop teasing his brother. Then she settled in for an evening of learning about Native Americans and their teepees. And that was Kristy's big night with a celebrity!

CHAPTER 4

"Your kisses are so sweet, your lips are like honey," I sang, as I got out of the shower. I was in a good mood, since my clock radio had woken me that morning by playing my favorite new song. Don't you think it's, like, a good sign when that happens? I do. "We're so in love, we won't need any money," I went on, as I gazed into my closet. I know the words to that song are dumb, but it has a catchy melody — one you sing all day and can't get out of your head.

Sometimes I wish I were the kind of person who thinks ahead about what I'm going to wear to school each day. Like Mary Anne. I happen to know that she lays out a whole outfit — from headband to shoes — each night before she goes to sleep. She is *so* organized.

But sometimes I'm glad I'm a disorganized slob at heart. I think the outfits I put together spontaneously are much more creative and fun than they would be if I planned each detail ahead of time. For instance, as soon as I looked in my closet that morning, I knew I wanted to wear this pair of black-and-white-checked stretch pants I just bought. I grabbed them and pulled them on. Next I started to look around for my red belt, since it would look perfect with the black and white. "I know it's here somewhere," I muttered as I poked around in my closet. Then I remembered: I'd been using the belt to hold my portfolio shut. The portfolio clasp was broken, but the belt held it together just fine. I found the portfolio under my bed and unbuckled the belt. I reminded myself to ask Mom for something to take the belt's place.

Next I needed a blouse. I figured a black one *or* a white one would look fine, so I knew I'd have no problem finding something. But I was wrong. Believe it or not, every one of my black blouses *and* every one of my white blouses was in the dirty laundry. Or crumpled at the bottom of my closet, which was basically the same thing.

I shrugged. Okay, I thought, no problem. I remembered that fashion magazines always say to be bold and mix your patterns. That's what I'd do! I checked the closet again and found a black shirt with white polka dots. I held it up and looked in the mirror. The dots next to the checks made me a little dizzy, but I decided that the total effect was just what I had been looking for. I pulled on my red ankle boots, put my hair into a ponytail on the side of my head (fastened with a black-and-white barrette), stuck on my favorite red heart-shaped earrings, and I was ready to go. All in under half an hour. That's how I get dressed almost every morning. I'm sure watching me do that would drive someone like Mary Anne nuts, but personally I think it's a lot of fun. It's always a challenge to come up with a super-cool outfit on the spur of the moment.

I grabbed my notebook and my shoulder bag and headed downstairs, humming as I went. "Something smells wonderful!" I said, as I hurried into the kitchen. "What's for breakfast?" I sat down at my usual place.

"I picked up these cinnamon rolls on the way home from work last night," answered my dad. "They looked so good I couldn't resist. They *are* good, too. Especially since your mom warmed them up in the oven. Try one." He pushed the plate over to my side of the table.

I took one and bit into it. "Mmmm," I said. "Yummy. Almost like junk food for breakfast."

Dad laughed. "The more it tastes like junk

food, the more you like it," he said, shaking his head.

"Hey, where's Janine?" I asked. I'd suddenly realized she wasn't at the table. That was weird. Janine is *always* on time. "Punctuality is an expression of consideration for others, Claudia," she says, whenever I'm five minutes late for anything.

"I'm sure she'll be down any minute," said my mom. She didn't look up at me; she was going over a report that she had to give that day. "Be sure to save her a roll."

I pulled my hand back from the plate. I'd just been about to take the last one. How does Mom *know* things like that? I glanced at the clock. "Well, if she doesn't hurry, she's going to miss the bus," I said.

"I'm sure she'll make it," replied Mom calmly. "Janine never misses the bus."

It was true, too. Perfect Janine. She never misses the bus, her homework is always done on time, and probably if she wanted to wear a white blouse one would be hanging neatly in her closet.

"Good morning, everyone," said Janine, as she slipped into her seat at the table.

"Morning, honey," said my mom, still not looking up from her report.

"Good morning, Janine," said my father, who was just finishing the crossword puzzle in the newspaper. He didn't look up either. "Have a roll," he added.

"Good m — " I stopped short as I took a look at Janine. I could hardly believe my eyes. Janine was, as usual, dressed in a gray kilt, a pale-blue button-down shirt, and a gray crew-neck sweater. (I would fall asleep immediately if I ever put on such boring clothes.) But something was very, very different about the way she looked that morning. It was her eyes. Or, to be more specific, her eye*lids*. They were covered with blue eyeshadow. This was the first time I had *ever* seen Janine wearing any kind of makeup. And it was pretty obvious that she wasn't used to it. She kept blinking and squinting, as if she had something in her eye. Plus, I think she had just smeared the stuff on without rhyme or reason; it didn't do anything for her looks, believe me. "Janine, I — " I was just about to point out that her makeup was smeared, when she reached for the roll I'd left her, and I saw something else that made me gasp.

Janine was wearing nail polish. It was applied about as well as her eyeshadow was, and the orangey color she'd chosen clashed horribly with her outfit, but there it was. Nail polish. On Janine. I opened and closed my mouth a few times, but no sound came out. I was speechless.

But Janine wasn't. "Mom, Dad, I just want to let you know I'll be late for dinner tonight," she said. "I have to go to the college library to work on a paper."

"That's fine, honey," said my mom. She glanced up at Janine, and I saw the shock in her eyes when she noticed my sister's makeup. But she didn't say anything. And she shot a Look at dad, warning him to keep quiet, too. My parents are pretty good that way; they don't make rules about what we can wear, and they hardly ever comment on the wild outfits I've been known to come up with. I guess my mother sensed that Janine didn't want to hear anything about the makeup she was wearing.

"Fine, honey," echoed my dad.

How about that? My parents trust Janine so much she doesn't even have to *ask* permission to be late for dinner. She just *announces* it. And they accept it. I don't think I could get away with that. But then, I don't have Janine's spotless record.

I got up to put my plate and glass in the sink. "You know I'll always stay, 'cause I love it when you look at me that way," I sang. The song was stuck in my head. It would be with me all day.

Janine looked at me and frowned. "Why are you singing that song?" she demanded.

"What?" I asked.

"What do you mean by singing that song?"

"I — nothing," I said. "I heard it on the radio this morning, and I can't get it out of my head. It's really catchy. Especially the part that goes, 'So I'll love you forever, forever I'll love you.' I like that part, don't you?"

Janine was glaring at me. She didn't answer. I guess I had been rambling a little.

"Well, I have to catch a bus," I said quickly. I grabbed my stuff and headed out the door without looking behind me. " 'Bye, everybody!" I called over my shoulder as I left. Out on the sidewalk, I shook my head. What a weird morning.

That day, at lunch, I told Stacey about Janine's strange behavior. " . . . and she was wearing *nail polish*!" I said as I peeled an orange.

"So what's the big deal?" asked Stacey. "I mean, I know Janine doesn't usually wear makeup, but after all, she *is* sixteen. Maybe she finally decided to look a little more sophisticated."

"It's not just that," I said. "She was late for breakfast, too."

Stacey giggled. "She's just going *wild*!" she said. "I'd call the cops if I were you."

"It's not funny," I said. But suddenly, it was. I imagined the police taking mug shots of Janine and booking her for "incompetent

35

makeup application," and "meal tardiness." I giggled. Stacey giggled. Soon we were completely hysterical.

That night, I helped my mom make dinner, something I hadn't done in a long time. I'm often busy with art lessons or a sitting job, so Janine usually helps out in the kitchen. "This is fun," I said, as I scraped carrots for a salad. "It reminds me of how I used to help Mimi make dinner." Mom and I smiled sadly at each other. Mimi was my grandmother — mom's mother — and she used to live with us. She died not long ago, and I miss her all the time.

Dinner was ready by six-thirty, but we waited until past seven to start eating. We were waiting for Janine. Finally, I couldn't wait anymore. "I'm starving," I said. "Is it okay if I have just a little stew?"

"Go ahead and eat," replied Mom. "I'd join you, but I don't seem to have much of an appetite. I'm worried about Janine."

"I'm sure she's fine," said my father, helping himself to a bowl of stew. "She did tell us she was going to be late, remember?"

"Of course I do," said my mother. "I just didn't think she'd be *this* late."

Guess what time Janine finally got home? Eight-*thirty*!

"Where have you *been*?" cried my mother,

when Janine walked in. "I was just about to call the police."

I thought of my lunchtime discussion with Stacey, and a giggle flew out of my mouth before I could stop it. My father frowned at me. Then he turned to my sister. "Janine, your mother was very worried about you," he said to her. "Please assure us that this won't happen in the future."

Janine apologized and promised she'd never be late again. I thought she'd be upset since our parents were so mad at her, but it didn't seem to bother her much at all. Humming that silly song from the radio, she rummaged around in the fridge and found some food. Then she headed upstairs to her room.

I stayed downstairs and watched TV for a little while since I had finished my homework, but soon I decided I was sleepy and ready for bed. As I climbed the stairs I noticed some movement at the end of the upstairs hall. It was Janine. She was walking quickly toward her room — and she was coming from the direction of *my* room.

"Hey!" I said. But she didn't seem to hear me. She hurried into her room and shut the door firmly behind her. I ran to my room and looked around. Once again, it looked messy — *different* messy. But I couldn't be sure that someone had been in there. And I couldn't figure out why Janine, of all people, would be sneaking around in my room. Something weird was going on, but I was too tired to figure it out that night. I fell asleep, and — would you believe it? — that song kept playing through all my dreams.

CHAPTER 5

When I woke up the next morning, the sun was streaming through my window. "Oh, no!" I cried, throwing off the covers. I jumped out of bed, grabbed my clock and shook it. "Eight o'clock! Why didn't the alarm go off? I'm going to be late for school."

I was in a total panic. I looked wildly around the room, trying to figure out what I should wear. This was no time for fancy outfits; I just had to get dressed as quickly as possible. I grabbed my jeans, which were draped over a chair. Then I turned to my bureau and started to open drawers and slam them shut. I was looking for my favorite red sweater, but it was nowhere to be found.

"*What* are you doing?" asked Janine. She was standing in the doorway, staring at me. She rubbed her eyes and yawned. She was wearing pajamas and a robe.

"What do you mean, what am I doing?" I

asked. "What are *you* doing? You're not even dressed yet. Oh, I don't believe it. How did we both manage to oversleep? You *never* oversleep." As I was talking, I was racing around my room, grabbing socks and shoes and trying to French braid my hair, all at the same time.

"Claudia," said Janine quietly. She had a funny little smile on her face. "There's something you may not realize." She paused for a moment.

"What?" I asked, as I hurriedly applied some mascara, smearing it in the process. *"What?"*

"Today is Saturday."

"Saturday?" I said, staring at her. I put down the lip gloss I'd just picked up.

"Saturday," Janine repeated. Then she cracked up, and so did I. "You should see yourself," Janine said. "You're wearing one red sock and one pink one. A big piece of hair is sticking out of your braid. You have black rings around your eyes, and your pajama top is still on."

"Hmm," I said. "All dressed up and nowhere to go." I threw myself on the bed, laughing. "I don't believe I just did that," I said. "All that running around for nothing." Then I remembered something. I had a sitting job over at the Pikes'. And I was supposed to be there at nine-thirty. So at least I hadn't gotten up early for no reason.

Janine was still standing in the doorway. "Um, Claudia," she said, sounding a little nervous. "I was wondering. Do you think I could borrow your red sweater?"

"My red sweater?" I asked, surprised. First of all, Janine never borrows my clothes. Secondly, if she did, I'd expect her to borrow clothes that were black, or brown, or navy blue. Janine never wears wild colors like red. "Well, sure," I said. "I guess so. Except I can't seem to find it."

"It's in my room," admitted Janine. "I — I saw it on top of the clean laundry pile, and all of a sudden I thought maybe I'd like to try it on. So I did." She sounded kind of defensive, as if she thought I was going to be mad at her.

"Well, I'm glad to know where it is," I said. "I thought it was lost. Sure, you can borrow it. But Janine, why — ?" I was about to ask her why she was acting so weird; why was she wearing makeup, and missing dinner, and stealing my clothes. But Janine had disappeared. I heard her call "thanks" as she headed back to her room, and I realized I'd lost my chance to find out what was going on with her. I shrugged. I couldn't wonder about it if I was going to make it to the Pikes' on time.

"Claudia's here! Claudia's here!" I heard footsteps running down the hall, *away* from the front door. I was standing outside on the porch. I'd rung the bell, and Claire, Mallory's five-year-old sister, had come to see who was at the door. She'd peeked through the window at me, and waved. I'd waved back. I could tell she was excited to see me. So excited, in fact, that she forgot to let me in.

I stood on the stoop for just a second, then let myself in. I'm no stranger to the Pikes, so I knew it would be okay. "Mal?" I called.

"In here," she yelled. Her voice was coming from the kitchen. "We're just finishing up the breakfast dishes."

As I approached the kitchen, I heard squealing and giggling and clattering sounds. The Pike family never does anything quietly. They can't, since there are so many of them. I poked my head into the kitchen. The room was full of noise and activity — and kids. "Hi!" I said.

"Hi," said Mallory. "Boy, am I glad you're here. My parents had to leave early, so they've already been gone for half an hour. I was okay for a little while, but now I'm definitely ready for some help!"

"You should have called me," I said. "I would have come earlier."

"I know," said Mal. "But it's Saturday. I figured you'd be sleeping in."

I giggled. "Ordinarily I would have been," I said. "But you won't believe what happened this morn — "

I was interrupted by a loud crash. I turned to Nicky, Mal's youngest brother. He's eight. He looked down at the floor, where a pile of forks and spoons lay scattered, then glanced up guiltily. "I didn't mean — " he began.

"It's okay," I said. "Let's pick them up and put them back in the sink. I'll wash them again, and then you can dry them and put them away. Deal?"

"Deal," he said. "And this time I won't try to pick all of them up at one time."

I rolled up my sleeves and started to wash the silverware.

"So, what happened this morning?" asked Mallory, who was putting away the pots and pans.

"Well, I woke up in a total panic," I said, "because I thought — "

There was another crash. This time Byron looked up guiltily. "It was Jordan's fault," he said quickly.

"Was not," said Jordan. "Adam did it."

"No way!" said Adam. "It was Byron."

Adam, Byron, and Jordan are triplets. They're ten years old, and they are almost *always* getting into some kind of trouble. This time, though, Mal let them off the hook. "It doesn't matter who dropped the frying pan," she said. "Just give it to me, and I'll put it away." Byron handed it to her, looking sheepish. I realized I'd probably never get around to telling Mal about what had happened that morning, and decided to concentrate on finishing the cleanup, instead. After I had washed the last fork, I looked around to see what else needed to be done.

Vanessa, who's nine, was wiping the kitchen counters with a sponge. She looked dreamy, as if she were in another world. Vanessa wants to be a poet, and she's often composing sonnets in her mind. That probably explained why she'd already wiped the same counter about ten times.

Claire was helping Margo, who's seven, organize the cereal boxes as they put them back in the cabinet. "I think the Chex should go next to the Shredded Wheat, since they're both squares," she said.

"Uh-uh," said Margo. "The Chex go next to the Cheerios, since they both start with C."

"Just get them in there however you can make them fit," said Mallory. "We could have been done by now if you all didn't dawdle so much. It's already almost time for lunch."

"Lunch?" said Byron. "What are we having for lunch, anyway? Derek likes hot dogs, I think."

"Derek?" repeated Mallory.

"Yeah. He's coming for lunch," said Adam. "Didn't we tell you?"

"No, you didn't," said Mallory. "But that's okay. I'll be glad to see him."

"Me too," I said.

"Me three!" said Nicky.

"We *all* want to see Derek," said Jordan. "And maybe we can have Hershey's *Kisses* for dessert, right, guys?" He nudged Adam and Byron. They snickered.

"Uh-oh," said Mallory under her breath. We exchanged glances. Obviously the kids at school had found out about Derek's kissing scene. Mal and I had already heard about it from Kristy. I smelled trouble, and I could tell Mallory did, too.

"There's the doorbell!" said Jordan. "I bet that's kissy-face Derek right now." He ran to answer the door.

As soon as he'd left the kitchen, Byron and Adam grabbed Vanessa. "Are you ready?" Byron asked her. "Your *boyfriend* is here!"

Vanessa pulled away. "I'm not so sure about this," she said.

"Sure about what?" asked Mal. "Hey, you guys, what kind of plot are you hatching?"

Byron tried to look innocent as Jordan and Derek came into the kitchen. As soon as the other kids saw Derek, they were all over him.

"It's like he's magnetic!" I whispered to Mal. She nodded. After we'd said hello to Derek, we stood there, waiting to see what was going to happen next.

The triplets pushed Vanessa so that she was standing next to Derek. "Go ahead!" hissed Jordan.

After a moment of hesitation, Vanessa closed her eyes, pursed her lips and tilted her chin up. Derek gave her a funny look. Then Adam bumped Derek from behind, pushing him into Vanessa. "Hey!" said Derek. "What are you guys doing?"

Nicky and the triplets just giggled. I was beginning to catch on, and so was Mal, I think. But Derek caught on even quicker. "Oh, I get it," he said. "You're trying to trick me into kissing Vanessa." He shook his head. "You guys are so immature. Kissing a girl is no big deal. I've done it tons of times." Derek spoke with plenty of confidence, but he didn't fool me. I could tell he was embarrassed, and boasting just to cover up.

Mallory looked as if she were in shock. "You *have*?" she asked Derek.

"Sure," he said nonchalantly. "I'm an expert. I'll show you. Ready, Vanessa?" He grinned devilishly and started toward her. She shrieked and ran out of the room.

The triplets seemed awestruck, and so did Nicky. Claire and Margo gazed admiringly at Derek. Mal's mouth was still hanging open in surprise. But I folded my arms and looked straight into Derek's eyes, and when he looked back at me the truth was obvious. Derek had never kissed a girl in his life.

I winked at him, to let him know his secret was safe with me. Then I said, "Who's ready for lunch?"

The kids began talking and fooling around again. They forgot about kissing, at least for the moment. Derek gave me a grateful look, and I knew I had just made a friend for life.

CHAPTER 6

I was all set. Six boxes of beads were arranged on my desk, along with plenty of string and a couple of needles. I was planning to work on some necklaces and bracelets, and I was hoping to finish at least a few of them before the BSC meeting, which would start in about an hour.

I love to string beads. It's relaxing, because once you decide on your design, there's not much to think about. You stick the beads onto the needle and push them down the string, and that's it. I make beaded jewelry for myself, for friends, and even for some of the kids we sit for. This time, though, I was making it as a favor to my mother. See, she's the head librarian at the Stoneybrook Public Library. And recently the library's budget was cut. Mom has had to be really creative about raising money for things the library needs — like books. Her latest idea was to hold a crafts fair, at which local artists and craftspeople could sell their work. The library would keep most of the money, and the artists would get some nice exposure. I thought it was a great idea, and I'd offered to donate some handmade jewelry. I was going to do beadwork, and also make some papier-mâché jewelry. But as usual, I had procrastinated (that's a word my mother taught me a long time ago — she uses it often to describe what I'm doing) and now I was going to have to work like crazy to finish the pieces.

So there I was: blue beads on my left, red ones on my right, and black, white, green, and purple ones in the middle. I threaded a big needle and reached for a red bead. Just then, I heard a knock at the door. I groaned. "Who's there?" I asked. It would be just like Kristy to be early for our meeting.

"It's me, Janine. Can I come in?"

"Sure," I said. "I'm just making some jewelry."

Janine came into my room, shutting the door behind her. "Hi, Claudia," she said.

"Hi," I replied. "What's up?"

She sat down on my bed and stared down at her shoes. "Nothing, really," she said. "What's new with you?"

"Not much." I strung some blue beads, then glanced at her. She was frowning slightly, and she kept smoothing the bedspread, as if she were nervous. "Janine," I said. "What's the matter?"

"Nothing! I mean — well, I wanted to ask you a favor."

"If you want to borrow my red sweater again, you'll have to wait," I said. "It's in the wash."

"It's not that, although I *would* like to borrow it again sometime." Janine paused for a moment. "What I wanted to ask was — was —"

"Come *on*, Janine," I said. "Spit it out! It can't be that bad."

"Would you give me a lesson on how to apply makeup?" she asked, all in a rush. "And also some advice about clothes?"

I was in shock. I guess I should have seen it coming, but still, it felt so strange for my sister to come to *me* for something. She's never needed my help before.

Janine seemed to think I was going to say no to her. "Claudia, I hate to bother you with this, but I don't know who else to ask. None of my friends wear cosmetics or get dressed up. Besides, I've helped you with your schoolwork so many times. Couldn't you help me just this once?"

"Janine," I said. "Of course I'll help you. Don't be silly. But why — "

"Do me one favor," she said, interrupting.

"Don't ask me why, okay? Let's just say it's time for a change, and leave it at that." She gave me an intense look.

"Fine!" I replied. Wow. I was dying to know what was going on with my sister, but I could see she was not about to tell me. Anyway, I figured it certainly was time for a change. After all, Janine is sixteen, as Stacey had pointed out. "Well," I said, putting down my needle. "Let's see. Where should we start? Stand up, Janine."

She stood. I looked her over and took inventory: straight black hair, cut in an old-fashioned Dutch-Boy style. Black wire-rim glasses. Navy-blue crewneck sweater, worn over a white blouse with a Peter Pan collar. Pleated knee-length gray wool skirt. Gray knee socks. Brown loafers. In those clothes, she looked like a skinny twelve-year-old. "Oh, boy," I said, sighing. "We've got our work cut out for us."

"I don't want anything *too* wild," said Janine nervously.

I laughed. "Don't worry. We'll take it one step at a time." I grabbed her hand and pulled her over to the full-length mirror. "First of all, your clothes need a little pepping up. You can keep that preppie style if you want, but let's make it a little more interesting." I pulled a green-and-blue patterned sweater out of my bottom drawer, and a white oxford shirt out of the closet, then found a short black wool skirt I hardly ever wear. "Try these on," I said. "See, it's the same thing: sweater, blouse, skirt. Only a little more daring and a little more defined."

Janine stepped into the bathroom to change. She's shy that way. When she came out, she was grinning. "I like it!" she said. "I look really different, but I'm still comfortable. This is great!"

I studied her. "Not bad," I said. "But you're going to have to ditch those loafers. Brown doesn't work with that outfit. Here, try these." I tossed her a pair of short black boots, and she put them on. "Perfect!" I said. "Now, let's work on your hair and your face." I sat her down at my dressing-table and stood behind her so we were both facing the mirror.

Janine shook her head dismally. "I'm so plain," she said. "You got all the good looks in the family."

"No way!" I cried. "You're really pretty. You just need to play up your best features." I thought for a moment. "Have you ever considered getting contacts?"

"Oh, I don't think so," she said quickly. "I'm used to my glasses. I would hate to have to fuss with contact lenses."

"Okay," I said, sensing that it would be better not to push the issue. "So we'll stick with the glasses. I think the first thing we should do is get some of that hair out of your face." I picked up a can of mousse and spritzed some onto my hands.

"What are you — " Janine began, but before she could stop me, I'd slathered the mousse all over her hair. "Oh, no," she said.

"Calm down," I replied, giggling. "I promise I won't hurt you." I played around with different hairstyles: first I swept all her hair over to one side, then I slicked it all back, then I made a little ponytail high on top of her head. None of them seemed right, and Janine was beginning to look horrified. Finally, I just pushed her bangs over to one side, added a couple of colorful barrettes, and stepped back. "That's it!" I said. "It looks great."

Janine gazed into the mirror and turned her head from side to side. "It looks okay, I guess," she said. "But what was that stuff you used? Do I have to get some? Where do I buy it?"

I cracked up. Janine is so smart about some things, but in other ways she's like a child. "It's just mousse," I said. "It's in all the drugstores. You might want to get some gel, too."

Janine shook her head. "I'll never learn to

use all this stuff," she said. She checked her reflection again and touched her hair. "Hey, it's stiff!"

"Use your fingers to comb it out a little," I said. "It'll soften up. Look, there's really nothing to it. I'll help you again next time, but you'll be able to do it yourself before you know it." I realized I ought to keep Janine's new beauty routine very, very simple. She wasn't used to spending time on her appearance. While Janine played with her hair, I looked through my makeup and picked out some mascara, some blush, and a pinkish lip gloss that wasn't too dramatic.

"What about eyeshadow?" asked Janine.

I remembered the blue smears she'd had on the other day, and winced. "If you want it, I'll show you how," I said. "But I think maybe brown would be a better color for you." I told her to close her eyes, and I quickly made her up, telling her what I was doing every step of the way. "Okay," I said, when I was done. "Take a look."

She opened her eyes and peered into the mirror. "Is that *me*?" she asked. "I can't believe it."

She did look different. I was going to have to get used to the new Janine.

"Thanks a lot, Claud." She was still staring at herself. "Wow," she said, under her breath.

Then she stood up to leave. She seemed to be in a trance.

"Why don't you stick around for a few minutes?" I said, looking at the clock. "The club is meeting soon, and you could show everyone how you look."

"Club?" said Janine. "Oh, my gosh! You mean it's almost five-thirty?" She whirled around and checked the clock. "I have to go! I have to meet — I mean I have to be at the library!"

The library? Janine had been at the library every night that week. She'd been at the library the night she missed dinner. I know Janine's grades are important to her but *nobody* could have that much homework. "Janine," I said. "Where are you *really* going?"

"I can't talk!" she gasped. "I'm late. Thanks again — and 'bye!" She ran out of the room and after a moment I heard the front door slam.

A few minutes later, Kristy showed up. Stacey, Dawn, and Mary Anne were right behind her. And Jessi and Mal ran up the stairs at 5:25. I was mystified by Janine's behavior, so I grabbed the five minutes before our meeting to tell my friends about her strange behavior. I even told them that I suspected that *she* had been the person who had been "messing up" my room — not that I had any idea why she would do that. Stacey had heard some of the story before, but this time even she was impressed by how different Janine seemed. "What do you think is going on with her?" she asked.

"I bet she got offered a part in a TV commercial," said Jessi. "That happened to this boy I used to know. He was just walking down the street, and these people came up to him, and — "

"That's pretty unlikely," interrupted Kristy. "She's probably thinking about running for student council, and she wants a new image."

"What?" asked Dawn. "No way. She must be up for some academic prize, and she's trying to impress her teacher."

"Maybe she has a boyfriend," said Mallory.

I looked at Mallory and snorted. Stacey laughed, too. The idea of Janine in love was pretty ridiculous.

We talked about my sister until Kristy interrupted us to bring the meeting to order. Then we talked about her some more, between phone calls. But we could not figure out what was making Janine act so weird. And the mystery was beginning to drive me crazy.

CHAPTER 7

Sunday

You know what? Kids are pretty funny sometimes. I can't believe I ever acted as silly as some of the kids we sit for — but I guess I did. In fact, I remembered this time when I was in second grade and I convinced myself that I was actually a princess, but that story doesn't really belong here. What I started to write about was what happened yesterday when I was sitting for Derek and Todd Masters. It was a Saturday, and we were just hanging around the house.

Stacey had tried to interest the boys in some kind of activity; a walk, a trip to the playground, an art project. But they vetoed every idea she came up with.

"It's been a long week," said Derek, sighing. "Now that it's over, I just want to relax."

Stacey couldn't help giggling. Derek sounded like some forty-five-year-old guy with a job and a mortgage on his home.

"What?" he said, when he noticed her laughing.

"Nothing. But I would think school would be a breeze after the way you work when you're in L.A."

"School, a breeze?" asked Derek, raising his eyebrows. "Not for me! I mean, I like it okay and all, but boy, these Stoneybrook teachers give a lot of homework."

"Hmm. Well, do you have any this weekend?" Stacey asked. "Maybe I could help you with it."

"Uh, no," said Derek quickly. "That's okay. Really."

Stacey frowned. She noticed that Derek and Todd kept exchanging glances, whenever they thought she wasn't looking. She decided to ignore their mysterious behavior and just hope it would stop soon.

"So, how about if I fix us a snack, you

guys?" she asked. She was pretty sure they wouldn't turn down *food*.

"Sure!" said Todd. "Can I have a Popsicle?"

"He won't eat anything but Popsicles anymore," said Derek. "Really! That's practically all he eats."

Stacey looked at Todd. He seemed healthy enough. "Well, if that's what you want, that's what you'll have," she said to him. "How about you, Derek?"

"Maybe a bowl of cereal. But I can get it myself."

Stacey led the boys into the kitchen. "What flavor do you want?" she asked Todd.

"Blue!" he answered.

Stacey laughed. "Is blue a flavor?" she asked. "Or a color?"

"Both," said Derek. He was pouring milk into a huge bowlful of Cheerios. "Those Popsicles don't taste like any certain flavor. They just taste blue."

Stacey hadn't had a Popsicle in years (because of her diabetes) but she kind of remembered what Derek meant. "I guess you're right. One blue popsicle, coming up!" She opened the freezer and found the box. Just then, the phone rang.

"I'll get it!" cried Todd.

"No, I will!" shouted Derek.

"You're both wrong," said Stacey. "I'll get

it." When we're baby-sitting, we try to be the ones to answer the phone, so we can take a message, if necessary, and also so little kids don't tell strangers that "mommy and daddy aren't home."

"Hello?" Stacey said, panting a little. She'd had to race the boys to the phone. "Oh, hi, Byron. Sure, he's right here. Hold on." She handed the phone to Derek.

"I knew it was for me," said Derek. He put the phone to his ear. "Hi, what's up?" He listened for a minute. Then he turned to Stacey. "Can those guys come over?"

"Which guys?" asked Stacey, teasingly. "Donatello and Michelangelo and Raphael and Leonardo?"

Derek rolled his eyes. *"Stacey!* You know who I mean. Byron and Jordan and Adam and Nicky. Can they come?"

Stacey hesitated. If the Pike boys came over, she'd be in charge of six kids altogether.

"We're just going to hang out in my room," Derek said. "I promise we won't get rowdy." He gave Stacey his most adorable Waldo-type look.

"Oh, okay," said Stacey.

"Yea!" yelled Todd, throwing his hands in the air. His blue Popsicle flew across the kitchen.

"Come on over," said Derek into the phone. He ducked as the Popsicle flew by him. "And don't forget to bring you-know-what." Then he hung up and grinned at Todd.

Stacey picked up Todd's Popsicle and rinsed it off. "Here you go," she said, giving it back to him. "Derek, why don't you finish your cereal before they get here?" She was curious about what "you-know-what" might be, but she knew better than to ask directly. She was already fairly certain that the reason Derek and Todd hadn't been interested in any of the activities she'd mentioned was because they'd had some sort of secret plans with the Pike boys. She decided to wait and see what happened.

Derek had just taken the last bite of his cereal when the doorbell rang. "They're here!" he said. He jumped up and ran for the door.

"Hold on," said Stacey. *"I'll* answer the door." She knew the Pikes were ringing the bell; she also knew it wasn't a good policy to let kids answer the door. When she reached the door, with Derek and Todd close behind her, she checked out the side window first. She couldn't see anybody. Our club has had some scary times with people who ring doorbells and then disappear. Then the bell rang again, Stacey looked more closely, and there stood the Pike boys. She opened the door. "Come on in, guys," she said. "How are you?"

"Fine," mumbled Jordan, squeezing past her. He seemed to be hiding something under his jacket.

"Fine," echoed Byron, Adam, and Nicky.

"See you!" said Derek, as all six boys took off for his room.

Stacey shrugged. She decided to let them enjoy being mysterious, as long as they played quietly. She figured she'd check on them every once in a while, just to make sure they weren't burning down the house. Meanwhile, she could sit on the couch and look through some of the extremely cool-looking fashion magazines that were arranged on the coffee table. We don't often get to take it easy during a baby-sitting job, and Stacey was only too happy to take advantage of the situation.

Stacey had relaxed for about five minutes when she heard the door to Derek's bedroom open and close. A second later, she saw Nicky tiptoe into the kitchen, holding a slip of paper. Then she heard him lift the phone off its hook and speak in a voice so low she couldn't hear what he was saying. He didn't talk long. After he'd hung up, he began to tiptoe back to Derek's room.

"Nicky," called Stacey. "Are you guys making phony phone calls?"

"No!" said Nicky. "No way. We've gotten into trouble for doing that before. We'll never do it again."

He sounded so positive that Stacey believed him. She also knew that if they *were* making phony calls, the other boys would be gathered around the phone while Nicky spoke, giggling and acting silly. (You might wonder how Stacey knew this. *I* wondered, when she told me about her day at the Masterses'. She wouldn't tell me, but I had a feeling she knew from experience.)

Anyway, Stacey let Nicky go back to Derek's room. And five minutes later, guess what happened? The same tiptoe-to-the-phone routine, only this time Adam was carrying the slip of paper and making the call. Stacey didn't even bother to question him, but she resolved to keep a closer eye on the boys.

She waited for a few minutes after Adam had returned to Derek's room. Then she snuck toward the closed door. She heard whispered conversation, but couldn't make out any actual words. However, the boys sounded awfully excited.

Stacey tapped on the door, and then opened it before they could answer. "Just a minute!"

Derek called out, but he was too late. Stacey saw Jordan shove something under the bed.

"What was that?" she asked. "Listen, you guys, I need to know what you're up to. I wouldn't want you to get yourselves in trouble." She bent down and looked under the bed. "A phone book?" she asked.

"Yeah!" said Adam. "It's just a phone book, that's all."

Stacey pulled it out. "This says 'Pike' on it."

"That's because it's ours," Jordan told her. "I brought it over."

Stacey remembered the bulge beneath his jacket. "What for?" she asked.

"Just to get some phone numbers," muttered Derek.

"For Becca and Charlotte!" cried Todd. Then he put his hand over his mouth. "Uh-oh," he said, looking guilty.

"That's all right, Todd," said Derek. "They're coming over, okay?" he asked Stacey.

"Well, it sounds as if you've already invited them, so I guess it's okay," said Stacey. "But next time you want to have a party, maybe you should let me — and your mom — know in advance."

Becca and Charlotte showed up soon after, and the kids moved into the rec room. Stacey tried to relax on the couch again, but the giggles and shrieks she kept hearing made her nervous. Finally, she pulled Todd out of the room and wormed the truth out of him.

"Lessons," explained Todd, after Stacey had grilled him for ten minutes. "Derek's going to give us kissing lessons, and Becca and Charlotte are going to help him dem — dem — "

"Demonstrate?" suggested Stacey. She wanted to laugh, but she realized she should control the urge. "I'm not sure that's such a great idea." She wondered what would happen if the kids' parents found out. She knew some adults might not think the situation was as hilarious as she did.

Stacey marched back to the rec room with Todd in tow, and broke up the party. "Okay, guys," she said. "And girls. Enough of this for today, I think. How about a game of Crazy Olympics instead?" She knew that the Pike boys, especially, could never resist *that* game, which they'd kind of invented. It involved coming up with all kinds of wild events, like the Pillow Jump, and then awarding prizes to whomever did them best.

The kids seemed to accept the change of plans. And Stacey couldn't help noticing that Derek looked especially happy — and relieved.

CHAPTER 8

I couldn't believe it. It boggled my mind. It flipped me out just to think about it. I never expected this to happen, not in a million years. Not to Janine.

Janine got grounded.

Perfect Janine, obedient Janine, Janine the *good* sister.

I knew I was wrong to feel happy about it. I tried not to show how I felt. But part of me was bursting with pure, wild joy. For once, I wasn't in trouble. For once, *I* could be the good sister.

Let me start from the beginning, since it will be a pleasure to tell the whole story again!

On Thursday morning, I was in the kitchen eating cinnamon toast. I was dressed and ready to go to school, so for once I could take my time eating breakfast. (I was wearing a royal-blue sweatshirt dress I'd just bought the day before.) I was talking to Mom about my plans for the weekend (sitting for the Perkins girls Friday night, going to the movies with Stacey and Dawn on Saturday night), and Mom was washing the dishes.

Then Janine came downstairs, wearing one of her new outfits — a gray wool skirt (one of her old ones, which she'd hemmed to a *much* more interesting length), a pink oxford shirt, which she must have bought recently, and my red sweater, which she seemed to have claimed as her own. Her fingernails were still orange. The pink and the red and the orange clashed just a little bit, but I didn't want to upset Janine by mentioning it. I had decided to encourage her fashion-wise and not pick on the little things.

When she sat down at the table, I could see that she'd also done her best with putting on some makeup. Her mascara was a little clumpy, and her blush wasn't blended as well as it could be, but overall she looked good. I gave her the thumbs-up sign, and she smiled.

She reached for a piece of toast and started to butter it. "Good morning, Mom," she said.

"Morning, hon," said my mother, who was still washing dishes.

"Where's Dad?" asked Janine.

"Oh, he had to leave early this morning."

Janine took a bite of toast and looked at Mom's back. "I won't be home for dinner tonight," she said quickly. "I'm going to be studying late again. I'll be at the college library, with a friend."

"Okay," said my mother. "It's all right for you to miss dinner now and then, as long as you tell us ahead of time. We just worry when we expect you and you don't show up."

Boy, Janine gets all the breaks. I'm sure I'd never hear the end of it if *I* wanted to miss dinner. Of course, I wouldn't be missing it in order to study. I'd probably be missing it because there was a special sale at the mall or something. And my parents just don't accept shopping as an excuse. I was all wrapped up in my thoughts, so I barely noticed when Mom asked Janine if she'd like to ask her friend over for dinner some time when they *didn't* have to study. "We'd love to have her," she added.

"Uh, sure," said Janine. "I will. Ask her, I mean."

It occurred to me then that Janine had been acting strangely throughout the discussion of her plans for the evening. I can't say exactly what tipped me off; maybe just the tone of her voice, or the way she was tapping her fingernails on the table. But all at once I knew Janine was hiding something.

My mom didn't notice. For one thing, her back was turned to Janine. For another, she just assumes Janine is always honest and reliable. But I knew. I hate to gloat, but I knew something was up. So I wasn't all *that* surprised at what happened a few days later.

It was Saturday. I was helping Mom with some yard work, which is not my favorite activity in the world. Mom was clipping the grass around the flower beds, where the mower doesn't reach, and I was following her with a rake. "You know," I said, "I saw this story in a magazine about these people who never, ever mow their lawn. It looks really cool — like a meadow. Why couldn't we do that?"

My mother sat back on her heels and wiped her forehead. "I never thought of that," she said. "It does sound like a perfect solution. But your father would not go for it. He kind of enjoys mowing the lawn."

"Just think, though," I said, beginning to imagine the possibilities. "We wouldn't have to rake leaves in the fall, because they wouldn't even show up in all that tall grass. And we'd probably find gorgeous wildflowers growing everywhere."

My mom shook her head. "It wouldn't work out," she said. "The neighbors would be furious with us."

"About what?" somebody asked. I looked up and saw Mrs. Braddock, who lives nearby. She had walked into our yard, carrying a big

69

basket. "It's hard to imagine being furious with the Kishi family," she went on.

Mom laughed. "Don't worry, we were just daydreaming," she said. She stood up and dusted off her knees.

"I brought you some bread," said Mrs. Braddock. "Haley and Matt and I have been trying to learn how to bake, and we ended up with more than we could ever eat."

"Isn't that nice," said Mom. I knew she didn't just mean it was nice of Mrs. Braddock to bring the bread. She also meant it was nice that she was spending time with her kids, learning how to bake bread together.

The Braddocks are a neat family. Our club baby-sits for them fairly often, so we know the kids pretty well. Haley is nine, and her brother Matt is seven. Matt is deaf. He can't hear at all. He communicates with sign language, which all of us club members have tried to learn. Jessi is especially good at it, but none of us is as good as Haley. She's fluent in it, and can have long, fast, complicated conversations with Matt. It's fascinating to watch them "talk." Their hands fly all over the place. In fact, they talk with their entire bodies.

"I haven't seen Matt and Haley for a long time," said my mom. "How are they?"

"Oh, just fine," said Mrs. Braddock. "And I can see that your kids are doing well, too.

Claudia, you look sophisticated even when you're gardening." I smiled. "And Janine is beginning to look like quite a young lady," Mrs. Braddock went on. "I saw her at Pizza Express the other night, and she looked radiant."

"Pizza Express?" my mother and I repeated "Janine?" my mother added.

"Mm-hmm," said Mrs. Braddock. "Let's see, it was Thursday night, I guess. The night before last. Yes, it was, because I was on my way to the movies. I waved at Janine through the window, but I guess she didn't see me."

My mother and I exchanged a look. "Well, I'm sure she didn't," said my mother. She and Mrs. Braddock talked for a while longer, and then Mrs. Braddock handed us three huge loaves of bread from her basket.

"I'd better go deliver the rest of these," she said, shaking her head. "We'll be supplying bread to the whole neighborhood for a while." She laughed.

Mom and I smiled and waved at her as she left the yard. But as soon as she was out of sight, Mom put down her hand and stopped smiling. "I can't believe it," she said quietly.

"What?" I asked, knowing perfectly well what she was talking about.

"It's just so unlike Janine to — " She stopped herself. "I'll have to talk to your father about this," she said, and I saw I wasn't going to get any more out of her. But I knew that *she* knew Janine had not told her the truth about Thursday night.

My dad returned from the golf course at about one that afternoon, and my mother grabbed him practically the second he stepped out of the car. She asked him to come into the house so they could talk. I stayed outside, raking, but I could hear their voices through the open kitchen window. Mom sounded pretty upset.

At three o'clock Janine came home from the library (at least, that's where she *said* she'd been), and that's when the fireworks started. This time, I could hear every word, since I was in the kitchen getting a snack. Mom and Dad nabbed Janine as she came into the house, and sat her down in the living room for a talk.

"It's not that we mind if you go to Pizza Express," I heard my mother say. "But the fact that you *misled* us, and said you were going to the library . . ."

Now, if *I* had been in that situation, I could have handled it much better than Janine did. I would have confessed to going to Pizza Express, since Mom had just said that she didn't mind that. But I would have said I had finished early at the library and decided to stop off for a slice on the way home.

Janine, however, doesn't have much practice handling parents. She's never had to fib, or make up white lies. She's always just been *naturally* good. So she blurted out the truth. "I *did* mislead you, and I feel terrible about it," she said. I heard her sniff, as if she were trying not to cry. "I just thought you wouldn't approve, that you wouldn't understand."

"Not approve of your eating pizza?" asked my father. "That's ridiculous. All teenagers eat pizza."

"I don't," said Janine miserably. "Or at least, I never did before. I was always too busy studying. And you're always so proud of how well I do in school. I don't want to disappoint you."

"Oh, honey," said my mother. "We care about *you*, not just your grades. And the only way you could disappoint us is by betraying our trust, which is what you've done."

I heard Janine sniff again. "I know," she said, in a tiny little voice. "I'm sorry."

"First you miss dinner and forget to call, and now this," my mother went on. "I'm afraid 'sorry' isn't enough."

"That's right," agreed my father. "But I think two days at home might teach you something."

"You mean I — I'm grounded?" asked Janine. She said the word as if it were in a foreign language, which in a way, it was — to her.

"Yes," said Mom firmly. "Your father and I agree that you should be grounded for two days. We're sorry to have to do this, but — "

"I understand," said Janine quietly.

In the kitchen, I put my hand over my mouth. I couldn't believe this was happening. Janine was being punished, and I wasn't! Not that it was all that much of a punishment. I mean, Janine spends most of her time studying anyway. Grounding her for two days wasn't going to change her life radically. Except that she wouldn't be able to go to the library, or Pizza Express for that matter.

Later that afternoon, I slipped into Janine's room to sympathize with her. "Tough break," I said.

"I deserved it," she replied. "I lied to them."

"But *why*?" I asked. "They don't care if you go out for pizza. They just said so."

"I don't want to talk about it, Claudia," said Janine stiffly. "Now, if you will excuse me, I have some homework to do."

That was it. I went back to my room in a huff, and right then and there I made a decision. I had not yet unraveled the entire mystery, and I was going to find out what Janine was up to. Then, maybe, if she was nicer to me, I could help her keep out of trouble. If not, at least I could satisfy my own curiosity.

I decided that the best way to find out what was going on would be to put a tail on Janine. A tail like in the detective stories. Someone who would follow her and observe her behavior. And who better to do that than the members of the BSC? Our club already has a great record in solving mysteries.

I reached for the phone and dialed Stacey's number. "Hi, Stace," I began. "You'll never believe what happened!"

CHAPTER 9

Stacey and I spent quite a while on the phone that night, plotting and planning. I also talked to Kristy, Dawn, and Mallory. When I woke up on Sunday morning, I knew that by then every member of the BSC must know about what had happened to Janine. And we were gearing up to find out what was behind her strange behavior.

I put on my robe and slippers and headed down the hall to Janine's room. "Hi," I said, rubbing my eyes and yawning. "Aren't you coming downstairs for breakfast?"

Janine was already up and dressed and hard at work on her computer. "I already had some yogurt and fruit," she said. "I decided that if I'm going to be stuck in my room, I might as well make the best use of the time."

Janine is unbelievable. Most normal average teenagers — like me — would never even think of "making the best use of the time" while they were grounded. I'll bet if you polled grounded kids about their main activities, "sulking" and "painting my toenails" would probably be high on the list. But Janine has never been normal or average. I don't know why I even expected her to act any differently than she always does. And trust me, it's not that unusual to find Janine doing homework at nine-thirty on a Sunday morning.

Sometimes it's so hard to believe she is actually my sister.

As I went downstairs, I felt my stomach begin to rumble. I could smell bacon frying and waffles cooking, and suddenly I was starving. "Morning!" I said to my parents as I entered the kitchen.

"Morning, sweetie," said my mom.

"Ready for waffles?" asked my dad, flipping a couple of them onto a plate.

"Definitely," I said. And then, for the next few minutes, I didn't say anything except maybe "yum" and "pass the butter, please." I was too busy stuffing my face with those delicious waffles. After the second one, I started to slow down. I was getting full. "I have to sit at the Masterses' later," I said to my mother, "but if you need more help in the garden this morning, I'm available."

My mother raised her eyebrows. "Thank you, honey. It's nice of you to offer," she said, sounding a little surprised. "But it looks like rain. I think I'll clean out the basement, instead."

"I could help with that," I told her. "After I clean up the kitchen, of course."

My mother looked kind of stunned. I don't usually offer to work around the house. I mean, I do the chores I've been assigned, but that's about it. And even then, to be honest, I often have to be reminded. No wonder my mom was surprised. But I guess she didn't want to look at a gift horse's teeth, or however that expression goes.

"Well, I'd be glad for your help," she said. "There's a lot to do."

I spent that morning being helpful and charming and polite, the "good sister." I only had two days to bask in the glow of my new status, so I wanted to make the most of it.

I could tell that my parents appreciated the new me, but I could also sense that they were a little bewildered about my sudden personality change.

The fact is, I'm the only one who worries about "good sister/bad sister." I know that, in reality, my parents love me and Janine equally. I know that they don't value her good grades over my artistic talent; both are given equal weight. And it's not that I'm a terrible person, or that I'm usually rude and lazy. My parents would probably think I was nuts if I explained what I was up to when I took on all those extra little jobs that Sunday morning. So I didn't explain. I just worked. And it felt good. But to be honest, I also knew I would be relieved when Janine's punishment was over and she could take back the "good sister" role. That's just the way my mind works.

Anyway, by that afternoon, I was already tired of being good. I don't know how Janine stands it! I was glad I had a sitting job, so I could get out of the house. In fact, I decided to walk over to the Masterses' instead of asking for a ride. That way I'd have to leave even earlier.

The sky was awfully gray when I stepped outside, but I didn't feel like going back in for an umbrella or a raincoat. I decided to chance it, even though it's a bit of a walk to the Masterses'. I walked quickly, thinking about what I might do that afternoon with Todd and Derek. I'd heard what our Kissing Expert had been up to lately, and I wanted to avoid any similar activities. I tried to think what else would interest the boys.

Suddenly, I realized something that made me smile. Derek might not really be a kissing expert, but he was an expert in something else: detective work! After his guest appearances on *Kid Detectives*, he probably knew all kinds of stuff about tailing people and cracking mysteries. He'd be *perfect* for helping me figure out the mystery at my house.

I ran the rest of the way to the Masterses', partly because I was excited and partly because it had started to rain. I was out of breath by the time I got there, but I managed to act professional with Mr. and Mrs. Masters. Then, as soon as they left, I pulled Derek and Todd into the living room. I knew Todd would probably be less interested in the Janine mystery than Derek would be, but I also knew Todd thinks anything his big brother does is fascinating.

"Listen, you guys," I said. "I want you to be my deputies."

"Do we get to wear stars?" asked Todd. I guess he's seen a cowboy movie or two on TV, so he knew just what a deputy is.

"Sure, I'll get you some stars," I said. "Now, Derek, I need your expert advice. You know a lot about how to be a detective, right?"

"Sure," said Derek. I had the feeling he was glad this conversation wasn't going to be about kissing.

"Okay, here's the situation," I said. I talked for a long time. I told the boys about Janine, and what she's like: How she never used to care about clothes or makeup. How she has no social life because her schoolwork comes

first. How she's always been a model child —
until now. And how she's changed.

Derek listened closely. "Wow," he said,
when I'd finished. "Something big is going
on."

"I know," I replied. "Do you think you can
help me find out what it is?"

"Definitely. It'll be a piece of cake."

"Cake!" said Todd. "*I* want some!"

Uh-oh. "Gee, I don't know if there is any,"
I said. "But come on, let's see what we can
find." Derek was already thinking hard about
The Case of The Weird Sister, so I figured I
better keep Todd occupied.

I took him into the kitchen and we looked
around in the breadbox, in the refrigerator,
and in the cupboards. I didn't see anything
even resembling a cake. "How about a
cookie?" I suggested.

"No!" cried Todd. "Cake!"

Four-year-olds can be very stubborn.
"Here's a nice banana," I said, picking one
out of a fruit bowl on the counter. "Wouldn't
you like a banana?"

"Cake," insisted Todd.

"But there isn't any cake. I was beginning
to panic. Any minute, Todd could throw a
tantrum. Then a light bulb went off in my
head. "How about a Popsicle?" I asked,
smiling.

"Yea!" said Todd. "A blue one!"

At that moment, Derek ran into the kitchen. "I've got it," he said. "Janine was abducted by aliens and brainwashed. Then they brought her back to Stoneybrook. She's like a totally different person now. That's why she's acting so strange."

"Derek," I said, "that doesn't sound like something you learned from *Kid Detectives*. That sounds like something you picked up from reading those magazines in the checkout line at the supermarket."

"Okay, okay," he said. "I've got another theory. How about this? Janine is a kleptomaniac. She's stealing all the time. She can't help herself, but she knows she should disguise herself when she goes into certain stores."

"Hmmm . . ." I said. "I like that idea a little better. It would explain the clothes and the makeup." Then I thought for a second, and realized it was ridiculous. A kleptomaniac? Janine? "I don't think so," I said.

"I could prove it if we could follow her," persisted Derek.

"Yeah, let's!" said Todd, licking his Popsicle and looking up at his big brother.

"Not today," I said. "It's pouring." It was, too. The rain was coming down in sheets outside the kitchen window. "Plus, Janine's grounded and she's not leaving the house to-day. Anyway, we need to think of some more realistic ideas about what she could be up to."

We spent the rest of the afternoon playing around with every wild and not-so-wild idea we could imagine. For every idea, Derek had a plan: how to follow Janine, how to catch her in the act, how to prove she was a bank robber, or a jewel thief, or whatever. I was impressed by how much Derek knew about detecting. Maybe we couldn't *do* much that rainy day, but we had a good time.

CHAPTER 10

Wednesday

Wow! Today's sitting adventure could have been an episode on Kid Detectives. Or better yet, a new show called Kid Detectives and Their Baby-sitters. We finally did some sleuthing today. We didn't exactly solve the Janine mystery, but we added one new clue to the story. Make that one big clue. One big, handsome clue.

Just as school was ending on Wednesday, Mary Anne reminded me that she would be sitting for Derek and Todd that afternoon. "I'm looking forward to it," she said. "Maybe we'll play detectives, since they seem to like that so much."

"Believe me, they do," I said. "Well, have fun. Say hi to Derek and Todd." I headed home. I was planning to work on stringing those beads again.

When I entered our house, I found Janine in the kitchen. She was eating rice cakes and reading a thick, boring-looking book. I pulled *my* after-school snack — a Devil Dog — out of my backpack, and sat down with the latest issue of *Seventeen*. Janine and I didn't seem to have much to say to each other lately. She wasn't ready — or willing — to tell me what she was up to, and I was tired of asking.

The kitchen was pretty quiet. "Is mom still mad at you?" I asked, finally. The night before, Janine had come home late for dinner again, and Mom had been furious. Janine hadn't been grounded this time, but I knew that, for her, Mom's being mad at her was almost worse.

"No, not really," said Janine. "I apologized again this morning, and she said she forgave me." She turned back to her book after she answered me, as if to let me know that she didn't want to talk.

I stood up, feeling a little mad at her, and went to my room. "Sisters aren't supposed to keep secrets from each other," I muttered to myself, as I set out my bead boxes. "Sisters are supposed to be best friends, and tell each other everything." But I knew that Janine and I were different. Oh, we get along most of the time. In fact, lately we've been getting along better than ever, except for the past couple of weeks. But the two of us are very, very different, and I know we always will be. So I had to get used to the idea that Janine wasn't about to tell me her secrets.

But boy, was I dying to know what they were! As I sat stringing beads, I couldn't stop thinking about what could possibly get perfect Janine in so much trouble. "Green, white, blue," I said out loud as I strung. "Green, white, blue." Then suddenly I threw down the necklace. I couldn't take it anymore! Janine's secret was making me crazy. I grabbed the phone and dialed the Masterses' number. "Mary Anne," I said, when she answered, "it's me, Claud. Can I come over?"

"Sure," she said. "We're kind of bored."

"Perfect," I said. "I know just what to do about that!"

I raced over to the Masterses' house and

banged on the door. Mary Anne, Derek, and Todd let me in, and immediately I began talking. "Okay," I said. "Here's the situation. Janine is at home now, but my bet is that she won't stay there much longer. Are you guys ready to tail her?"

"Yeah!" yelled Derek and Todd.

"Um, okay," said Mary Anne, a little nervously. "But what if she sees us?"

"She won't," said Derek, sounding confident. "I know all the tricks. Just watch me and do what I do."

"Are we ready to go, then?" I asked.

"Just a minute," said Derek, holding up one finger. He ran to his room. When he returned he was wearing a hat like the ones detectives wear in old movies. "I got this when I was on the show," he said proudly. "The director gave it to me."

"Nice," I said. It really was a neat hat. The only thing was that it didn't exactly make Derek look inconspicuous. You don't see too many eight-year-olds in fedoras wandering the streets of Stoneybrook. But it didn't matter. If Derek wanted to wear the hat, it was fine with me.

"Let's go!" he said.

Mary Anne glanced at me and started to say something. "Maybe we shouldn't — "

"Oh, come on, Mary Anne," I said. "It's

just for fun. We'll have a good time!" Sometimes Mary Anne is too timid for her own good.

"Yeah, come on!" said Todd, grabbing her hand. Derek took her other hand and gave her that Waldo grin.

"Oh, all right," said Mary Anne. She couldn't help grinning back at Derek. "But I hope you really do know what you're doing!"

"Trust me," he said as he led the way out the door and down the street.

We walked all the way around the block, so we could approach my house from the side where the bushes are the tallest. (That was my idea.) When we got there, Mary Anne and Derek and I squatted down. Todd didn't have to squat, since he's still pretty little. "Shhh!" said Derek, putting his finger over his lips. "Now we just wait for a while. This is called a stakeout."

"Are we having a barbecue?" asked Todd.

We were all confused for a minute. Then I giggled. "Not steak like meat," I said. "This is different. We're watching for Janine to come out of the house." Mary Anne and Derek were giggling, too. We put our hands over our mouths to muffle the sound.

"Oh," said Todd. "Well, isn't that her?" He pointed toward the front door. Janine had just walked through it!

"Oh, my lord!" I whispered. I ducked down to make sure I was completely hidden, and pulled Mary Anne along with me. "What's she doing?" I hissed to Derek.

"Looks like she's waiting for somebody," he whispered. "She keeps looking down the street."

I peeked through the bushes. Janine was standing on the front steps, and sure enough, she was watching for *something*.

"It's the mailman," whispered Mary Anne suddenly. She sounded excited. "That's who she's waiting for," Mary Anne's eyes were bright. She certainly wasn't feeling timid any more.

"You're right," I whispered, after I'd taken another peek. "The mailman's here. She's taking the mail from him, she's looking through it — "

"And she's putting a letter into her pocket!" said Derek, a little too loudly.

"Shh!" Both Mary Anne and I turned to him with our fingers over our lips.

"Sorry," he whispered, looking sheepish.

By then, Janine had turned and gone back inside. She didn't seem to have heard a thing.

"Wow," said Derek. "That was good stuff. I'd do just about anything to get my hands on that letter! I bet it would tell us everything we need to know."

"Maybe," I said. "But I'm not about to steal Janine's mail."

"Yeah, right," said Derek, looking disappointed. "Oh, well. I guess we just wait some more, then."

We settled in behind those bushes. Derek kept an eye on the house, but Janine seemed to have settled in, too. There were no signs of activity. After a while, Todd started to get squirmy; it's hard for a four-year-old to sit still for very long. "Todd," I heard Mary Anne whisper (he was sitting on her lap), "can you say your alphabet for me?" That kept him occupied for a few minutes. Then he made up a song about numbers, colors, and shapes. Soon, though, Mary Anne began to run out of ideas. She was beginning to seem a little desperate, when Derek suddenly sat up straight.

"There she is!" he hissed. "She sure looks different, though."

"Wow," breathed Mary Anne, peering through the bushes. "I'll say. She looks almost like — "

"Claudia," Derek chimed in.

I had been trying to get a look, but my foot had fallen asleep and I couldn't get up. Finally, I peered through the bushes from where I was sitting. "Hey! That's my red sweater," I said.

"Shhh!" said Derek and Mary Anne.

"Sorry," I said, covering my mouth. But it was true. Janine was wearing my sweater *again*.

"Boy, I see what you mean about the makeup," whispered Mary Anne, turning to me. "She's putting on a lot of it these days, isn't she?"

I nodded. "I keep trying to tell her that subtle is better, but she can't seem to get the hang of it." Even from where I was sitting, I could see Janine's red lipstick and blue eyeshadow.

"Okay, time to move out," said Derek suddenly. Janine had turned right at the end of our driveway, and was walking quickly down the street. "She looks like she's on her way to meet somebody," Derek went on. "She keeps checking her watch."

Mary Anne and I glanced at each other, impressed. Derek was pretty good at this!

We followed Janine as she walked down Bradford Court. It wasn't easy to keep ourselves hidden while we kept Janine in view, but we managed. Mary Anne was carrying Todd piggyback, since he's kind of a slow walker.

"Want me to take a turn?" I asked.

"I'm okay for now," she said. "He's light."

"Turning!" said Derek. Sure enough, Janine had turned left off Bradford, and then, after checking the traffic, she'd crossed the street and taken a quick right onto Rosedale Road.

"She must be going back to school for something," I said. I was disgusted. As if Janine doesn't spend enough time at Stoneybrook High. Now she had to drag all of us there, too. Then I realized that I was being ridiculous. After all, we'd chosen to follow her!

"Aha!" said Derek. "See? What did I tell you? There's the person she's meeting."

I looked, and my mouth dropped open. There, in front of the school, was the most gorgeous guy I've ever seen. He was tall and strong-looking. He had black hair, and he was dressed in a way cool pair of jeans and a beautiful blue shirt.

"That can't be one of Janine's friends," I said. "He doesn't have a plastic pen-holder in his pocket, or a slide rule in his hand."

But Janine walked right up to him. They shook hands and smiled at each other. Then they started to walk away together — and they *didn't* go into the school!

"Claudia!" I heard Mary Anne's voice as if it came from a great distance. I was still staring at Janine and that hunky guy. "Claud, I hate to say this, but it's after five! We have to get the boys home and then get to the BSC meeting. Mrs. Masters promised to be home by five-twenty."

I couldn't believe it. We had to leave, just when things were really starting to happen. What could Janine possibly be doing with a boy like that? I was mystified — frustrated, too. I wanted to solve the mystery *now*!

"He really was *very* good looking," said Mary Anne. "You guys would have thought so, too."

It was about 5:45. We'd taken care of all the club business during the first few minutes of our meeting, and then I'd filled everyone in on the latest news on Janine. Mary Anne had added a few comments here and there, to back me up.

"This is so awesome," said Mallory, who was sitting cross-legged on the floor next to Jessi. "Do you think that guy is some kind of spy or something? Maybe Janine is passing secret results to him. She's always working in the chemistry lab, isn't she?"

"Well, yes," I said. "But it's hard to imagine that there'd be any major scientific break-throughs in the chem lab at Stoneybrook High."

"You never know," said Mal.

"She's right," agreed Jessi. "The other day I was reading about this discovery made by a kindergarten teacher in Louisiana — "

Just then the phone rang. I was so involved in our conversation that I'd almost forgotten the reason we were gathered in my room. Kristy was leaning back in her director's chair, but she rocked forward and grabbed the phone. "Hello, Baby-sitters Club. Can I help you?" Kristy's always so businesslike. "Well," she said, after she'd listened for a moment. "Normally the jobs just go to whoever is free. But I think in this case that can be arranged. Why don't I call you back as soon as we've checked those dates?"

Kristy hung up and turned to me. "That was Mrs. Masters. She said she needs a sitter for Thursday and also for Saturday, and that Derek has asked especially for you."

"I guess he's just as curious about Janine as we are, by now," I said. "He probably wants to stay on the case until it's solved. And I could sure use his help. He really is a good detective."

"Is this all right with everyone else?" asked Kristy. She looked around the room.

Jessi and Mal nodded. Stacey gave the thumbs-up sign. "Fine with me," said Dawn. "Just as long as you keep us posted on the mystery."

Mary Anne checked the record book. "You're free," she said to me.

"Okay, then," said Kristy. "Claud, go ahead and call Mrs. Masters."

While I made the call, the others started talking about my sister again. When I hung up, Stacey turned to me. "What are you going to do now that you know more about Janine's secret?"

"I'm not sure," I replied. "For one thing, I still don't really know what her secret *is*. For another thing, I'm not about to tell my parents what I saw. They'd just be mad at me for spying and sneaking around, and anyway, I don't believe in ratting on people."

"Maybe you should approach Janine and tell *her* what you know," said Dawn. "Then you could ask her to explain why she's meeting that guy."

"No way," I said. "I've tried asking her questions. She just freezes up. I think we're stuck. We started out being sneaky, and now we have to keep being sneaky."

"Hmm," said Jessi. "Well, I guess Derek's the best person to help you, in that case."

"But we can't just keep following her around," I said. "She's bound to catch us if we do that."

"You need a plan," said Dawn, rubbing her

hands together. "Let's figure out a good one."

"You're sitting for Derek on Thursday, right?" asked Stacey. "Well, what if you thought up some reason for Janine to have to come over to the house — "

"Like saying Derek needed help with his homework?" I asked eagerly. "Great idea. Janine's helped me out like that before, so she wouldn't suspect a thing."

"Right!" said Stacey. "Then, once she's there, you and Derek can trick her into talking. About her secret, I mean."

"How do we do that?" I asked. That part of the plan sounded tough. Everybody else seemed to think so too, since the room was silent for a few moments.

"I know!" said Kristy, suddenly. She leaned toward me and started to talk in an excited voice.

"Hi, Janine?" I said, into the phone. "It's me, Claud." My heart was beating fast. Derek, who was standing beside me, made an encouraging face. "Listen, I've got a problem. I'm sitting over at the Masterses'. And Derek has this civics homework that's giving him a lot of trouble, and I can't figure it out either. So I was wondering — " I stopped to listen for a second. "You will?" I asked. "Really?

You don't mind?" I grinned at Derek. "Okay, we'll see you soon, then." I hung up, and Derek held his hand out for a high-five.

"All *right*," he said. "She's on her way!"

I nodded. "She must feel guilty for being so cold to me recently. She said she'd be right over."

"Okay, let's get set up," said Derek. He had understood Kristy's idea right away, and he couldn't wait to try it. "Remember, just follow my lead and this is guaranteed to work. You too, Todd," he said to his little brother. "Just do whatever I tell you, okay?"

"If I do, you'll let me play with your G.I. Joe, right?" Todd asked. "You promised."

"That's right," said Derek. "You can play with my Turtles, too. Just do what I tell you." Derek had led me and Todd into the rec room by then. "Now, let's see," he said. "I *think* if we move these two chairs over there, and set up the TV table as kind of a podium — "

The doorbell rang then, and I ran to answer it. "Hi, Janine," I said, as I let my sister in. "Thanks for coming. The boys are in the rec room." I was pretty nervous. My heart was beating like a drum, and my palms were sweaty. But if Kristy and Derek thought the plan would work, who was I to question it? I pointed Janine toward the rec room and then stopped in the bathroom to splash some cold water on my face.

"So, the thing is," Derek was saying when I joined them in the rec room, "I'm supposed to stage a courtroom drama, and then write up what happened. We're studying the legal system, and my teacher wants to make sure we understand it."

"Sounds like fun," said Janine. "How can I help?"

"Well, I thought you could act out one of the parts, and also kind of guide us through the process," said Derek.

"I don't know," said Janine. "I mean, I'm glad to help, but I don't know that much about legal procedure. I've only taken a couple of courses in it."

"Well, you know more than I do," Derek assured her. "Me and Claudia know some stuff from watching *Citizens' Court* on TV, so between us, we should be okay."

"Claudia and I," said Janine.

"Claudia and you what?" said Derek.

"You said 'me and Claudia,' " said Janine. "You should have said 'Claudia and I.' "

"Oh, right." Derek was smiling. "Whatever you say." He raised his eyebrows at me, and I gave him a little smile and a shrug. "Okay, let's get started," he said. "Todd, I think you should be the judge. Janine and me can be witnesses, and Claudia can be a lawyer."

Todd picked up the hammer from his Lil' Carpenter set and started to bang on the TV stand. "All rise, please," he said.

I giggled. "I guess he's watched Citizens' Court, too," I said.

Janine was just standing there, frowning. "Janine and I," she said.

"What?" asked Derek.

"Not 'Janine and me,' " she said. " 'Janine and I.' "

"Oh, right," said Derek. "Sorry." He turned to pick up a pad of paper and some pens.

"Janine," I whispered. "He's only a little kid. If you correct him every time he makes a grammatical mistake, we'll never get finished."

She nodded. "All right. I'll try to resist the impulse."

Derek handed me the pad. "Okay, Ms. Lawyer," he said, grinning. "Let's get started."

In case you're wondering, Kristy's idea had been to set up this courtroom atmosphere in order to force Janine into telling us her secret. She figured that enough talk about truth and honesty would cause Janine to break. So now it was up to me to get the ball rolling.

"Ms. Kishi and Mr. Masters," I said. "This court is now in session. You are both extremely important witnesses. Have you been sworn in yet?"

They shook their heads. "Is this really necessary?" asked Janine. "Maybe you should just get started on telling us about the plaintiff and the defendant."

"No!" said Derek. "We have to do it right, or else it won't count."

"Oh, all right," said Janine.

"Put your hands on this book," I said, holding out a copy of *Charlotte's Web*. Janine and Derek touched the book. "Do you swear to tell the truth, the whole truth, and nothing but the truth?" I tried to sound very serious, and kind of threatening.

"I do," said Janine, smiling.

"I do," said Derek. He sounded subdued all of a sudden, and he looked very nervous.

Todd was sucking on the end of his hammer. "Okay, judge," I said to him. "We're ready to start the questioning."

"I think you're supposed to call him 'Your Honor,' " said Janine.

"Oh, right," I said. "Anyway, here goes. First, I want to repeat how important it is for you both to tell the truth. Remember, once you begin to tell lies, it's hard to stop." I glared at Derek and Janine. Derek had a funny look on his face. "Once you start to lie," I continued, "you keep digging yourself in deeper, and the lies begin to ruin your life. Lies are very, very dangerous." I looked straight at Janine as I said this, hoping to make an impression. But then I heard a strange noise, and I realized Derek was crying.

"I can't stand it," he said. "I have to tell somebody the truth. I told a lie and now it's ruining my life, just like you said."

"Derek!" I hissed. "What are you *doing*?" I nodded toward Janine.

"I don't care," he sobbed. "I just can't stand it for another minute. Here's the truth: I'm not a kissing expert. I haven't kissed lots of girls. In fact, I've never kissed a single girl in my life! And now I have to, and I'm scared."

I rolled my eyes. Derek wasn't telling *me* anything new. The members of the BSC had already figured out how scared he was, and why. Why did he have to pick *now* to break down? He'd blown our whole plan. Then I saw Janine kneel to hug him, and I felt ashamed of myself. Poor Derek! He'd really been suffering. I gave him a big hug, too, and I could see that on top of everything else, he was upset about ruining the plan. "It's okay," I whispered in his ear. "We'll get her some other way."

CHAPTER 12

I was so *frustrated* by how our plan to trap
Janine had failed. And what made things
worse was that Janine had no idea the afternoon had been a total waste. She kept saying
she was sure Derek had gotten some "wonderful material" for his class, and that she felt
sorry for Derek because his lies had gotten him
into such a mess. She didn't seem to realize
her lies had gotten *her* into a mess, too.

By Saturday, when I sat for Derek and Todd
again, I was sick of thinking about Janine and
her secrets. I just wanted to have a good time
playing with the boys, and to forget about
solving any mysteries. I'm not saying that I
wasn't still curious about Janine; I just needed
a day off. As I walked to the Masterses', I
resolved to spend the day simply having fun.

"Hey, guys," I said as I reached the Masterses' driveway. "You look like you're having
a blast." Todd was riding around on his little

bike, which has training wheels, and Derek was practicing moves on his skateboard.

"We are!" said Todd. "Look what I can do!" He zoomed up the driveway, made kind of a shaky turn, and zoomed back down.

"All right, *Todd*," I said. "You're a great bike rider."

"Check out *my* moves," said Derek. He stepped onto the skateboard and rocked it back and forth. "Just like the guys at Muscle Beach, right?"

"Where's Muscle Beach?"

"Oh, it's out in California," said Derek. "It's this place where all the coolest skaters go to show off their stuff."

"Neat," I said. "Hey, you guys go on riding. I'm just going to let your parents know I'm here." I knocked on the door, and Mrs. Masters answered it.

"Oh, hi, Claudia," she said. "Thanks for being on time. We're just about ready to go." She reached for her car keys. "The boys have been having such a good time with you," she said. "They really like that detective game you've been playing."

"Oh, right," I replied. "Well, I have fun with them, too." I wasn't about to tell her that playing detective was more than a game. She probably wouldn't like to know I was encouraging her boys to spy on people. All the more reason, I thought, to give the detective work a rest.

After the Masterses left, I sat outside on the curb and watched the boys ride around for a while longer. Soon, though, they wanted to do something else.

"Let's go see what Janine is doing," said Derek. "I bet we can crack that case if we follow her today."

"Yeah! Let's play spy," cried Todd. "I promise to be really quiet."

"Sorry, guys," I said. "I think we better leave Janine alone for a few days."

"I'm really sorry I messed up our plan," said Derek. "I can't believe I did that."

"Oh, Derek, that's all right," I replied. "I think you were under a lot of pressure about that kissing stuff. I just hope you feel better now that you've told the truth."

"Oh, I do!" he said, smiling. "I really do." Then his face clouded over. "But only you and Janine and Todd know the truth. I still have to figure out what to do about my friends."

"Well, I'm sure you'll do the right thing when the time comes," I said. "Now, how about a game? Let's see," I said, thinking. Sometimes it's hard to come up with games that will work for kids who are different ages. "I know!" I said, after a moment. "How about Animals?"

"Animals?" asked Todd. "How do you play that?"

"Well, I first pick an animal and pretend I *am* that animal. You two have to guess what I am. Whoever guesses first gets to be the next one to act out an animal."

"Cool," said Derek. He sat down on his skateboard, and Todd sat next to him.

"Okay," I said, thinking quickly. "Here goes!" I started to lope around, bent over, with my hands hanging down low. Once in a while I'd stop and scratch myself. I made little grunting noises, too.

"A gorilla!" yelled Todd.

I straightened up. "That's right," I said. "Your turn."

Todd thought for a second, and then started to run around the yard, barking like a maniac.

"Dog!" yelled Derek. Todd nodded, but he kept running and barking for a few minutes, enjoying being a dog. When he was done, Derek stretched his neck out as far as it could go. He made ears by holding his right hand behind his head. He looked kind of graceful, if you can imagine that.

That's when I realized that Derek really is a good actor. He's not just pretending to be Waldo on the show. This may sound corny, but the fact is that Derek has a special gift for actually *becoming* something or somebody else.

He'd chosen a hard animal to act out, but it only took seconds for me — and Todd — to realize what he was. I let Todd be the one to guess first.

"Giraffe!" cried Todd.

"That was great, Derek," I said.

Derek blushed. "Thanks," he said. "I like this game. I guess I miss acting sometimes."

We played a few more rounds, and then, just as Todd was being a very convincing penguin, I heard voices behind me. I turned around and saw all four Pike boys — and Vanessa — walking up the driveway.

"Hi!" called Nicky. "What are you guys doing?"

"Hi, Nicky," I said. I turned to Derek. "Didn't you and Stacey have a little talk about inviting kids over without checking with the baby-sitter first?" I asked.

"I didn't invite them!" cried Derek. He looked a little nervous, and I could guess why.

"We're here for a demonstration," said Byron.

"Yeah," said Adam. "A demonstration from an expert."

"Right," added Jordan. "An *expert* demonstration." The triplets folded their arms across their chests.

"Of kissing!" added Nicky, as if it were necessary. "And Vanessa's all ready to be kissed!"

I looked at Derek. He looked as if he'd rather be just about anywhere but his own driveway. "I think I hear the phone ringing," he said, desperately. He began to edge toward the front door.

"No way," said Byron, blocking his path. "We're tired of waiting. We want to see how you do it."

I had the feeling the Pike boys were testing Derek, as if they knew, somehow, that he'd been making up all those stories about what a great kisser he was. I stepped closer to the kids. "Okay, guys," I began. "Let's — "

"Wait a minute," said Derek. He took a deep breath. "There's something I have to say." He paused and looked at me.

I nodded at him, telling him to go on.

"I've never kissed a girl in my life," said Derek. He let out a big breath and looked around at the Pikes. "I'm no expert. I don't know anything at all about kissing. And I'm really, really scared about having to kiss somebody on the show." He hung his head, waiting for the teasing to start.

I held my breath.

Byron stepped forward. "Hey," he said, slapping Derek on the back. "We knew it all along!"

"Y — you did?" asked Derek.

"Well, maybe not all along," said Adam.

"But we *were* starting to wonder," said Jordan.

"Does this mean I get to go home?" asked Vanessa. She looked extremely relieved. "See you later!" She ran down the driveway.

"Hey!" yelled Byron. "You owe us money!"

"Yeah," shouted Adam. "You don't get to keep it if you didn't kiss him!"

Vanessa just kept on running.

"We put together all the money we had," Jordan told Derek. "We gave her two dollars and thirteen cents, just to kiss you."

Nicky looked disgusted. "Now we have to figure out how to get it back," he said.

"I bet we can come up with an idea," replied Derek. "Let's see . . ." He frowned, as if he were thinking hard.

"Come on, Todd," I said. "Let's you and I play Animals by ourselves." I figured we should let the boys be alone for a while. They could talk "boy talk" and patch up their friendship.

Todd and I left Derek and the Pike boys alone for the rest of the morning, and by lunchtime they seemed to have forgotten the Kissing Expert episode. Nicky and the triplets went home looking happy; they had figured out a foolproof plan for getting their money back from Vanessa.

"They're going to find some really ugly baby

pictures of her," explained Derek as I made the boys tuna fish sandwiches. "And they'll threaten to bring them to school and show them to everybody unless she gives the money back."

"That should work," I said, smiling. "So, is everything okay now?" I asked.

"Yup," said Derek. "I really learned a good lesson. You know, I think sometimes I lie when I feel nervous or upset about things. Remember when I first came back to school and I made up that story about a mean kid?"

I nodded.

"Well, that was just because I was nervous. But you know what? It didn't do any good to lie. Not that time, and not this time. I'm never going to lie again, I swear." Derek looked very, very serious.

"Boy, you really *have* learned a lesson," I said. "I'm proud of you. It must have been hard to tell the truth today, but you did it." I knelt down and gave Derek a hug.

"You helped me," he said. "You and Janine."

CHAPTER 13

"*Janine*?" I repeated. I couldn't believe my ears. Janine was the biggest liar in Stoney-brook these days. How could she teach Derek about telling the truth?

"Sure," said Derek. "She was so nice to me the other day. You know, when I began to cry during our pretend courtroom?"

"That's true," I admitted. I remembered the way Janine had hugged Derek.

"She made me feel like it was *good* to tell the truth. That's why I was brave enough to do it today." He smiled. "And it worked out really, really well. I can't believe how I lucked out. I thought the guys were going to be mad at me, but instead now they feel sorry for me because I have to kiss a girl!"

"Well, I suppose Janine does know that telling the truth is a good idea," I said. And then I remembered something I learned in school last week. I learned about this thing called irony. Irony's kind of like when something

111

happens that is the opposite of what you would expect. I'm certainly not explaining this well, but take it from me, it was very *ironic* that Janine would be the one to teach Derek about the benefits of telling the truth!

"You and Janine are the greatest," said Derek, interrupting my train of thought. "Will you tell her I said thanks?" Then he jumped up from the kitchen table. "Never mind, I'm going to do it myself, right this minute." He ran to the phone before I could stop him.

"Hey, Todd," I said. "Why don't you get your bulldozer and we'll go outside."

A few minutes later Todd was pushing his Tonka bulldozer around in a pile of dirt near the driveway. Luckily, he's the kind of kid who enjoys playing by himself, because lately he hasn't been getting much attention. I'd been too busy with Derek and his kissing problems and Janine and her secret. Todd just tags along. But he seems happy, so I decided I shouldn't worry.

"I'm making an airport," he explained. "So me and Derek can land our jet planes here." He made some bulldozer noises.

"Cool," I said, as Derek ran outside. "Hey, did you talk to Janine?" I asked.

"No, the line was busy," he said. "I tried three times!"

"That's funny," I said. "I'm the only one at our house who stays on the phone that long. Maybe you called the wrong number. What number were you dialing?"

Derek rattled off a number, and my mouth dropped open.

"That's *my* line!" I said. "That one shouldn't be busy. Nobody uses that phone but me and the members of the BSC."

"Well, somebody is using it right now," said Derek. "I'm sure that's the number I called."

"This is weird," I said. "Who — " Suddenly I realized who was using the phone. "Janine. It must be Janine!" I shook my head. What was she doing using my phone without permission? It made me mad — and very curious. I just had to find out who she was talking to. But then I remembered my resolution to forget about Janine while I was sitting for Derek and Todd. I could talk to her when I got home.

"Should we put a tap on the line?" asked Derek. He was standing next to me, looking as curious as I felt.

"No," I said, smiling. "This is my sister we're talking about, not a criminal, remember? Hey!" I cried, changing the subject. "Check out Masters International Airport over here!" I led Derek to where Todd was playing. "Look at this runway," I said. "This is going to be great."

That was all it took to distract Derek. After all, he's a kid first, even if he *is* also a TV star and a great detective. He knelt down in the dirt with Todd and spent the rest of the afternoon playing with his little brother.

It wasn't so easy to distract myself. As I watched the boys play, all I could think about was The Mystery Of Janine. What was she up to? Why was she lying to my parents? Who was that guy she had met? And why was she tying up my phone? Maybe it was time to confront her after all. I was going to tell her everything I knew, and I wasn't going to let her put me off or ignore my questions. I was going to get some answers.

I was all psyched up by the time I arrived home that afternoon. I ran right upstairs and knocked on Janine's closed door. "Yes?" she called.

"It's me, Claud," I said.

"What do you want?"

"I want to talk to you," I replied, staring at the closed door. This was so unlike Janine. Usually she leaves her door wide open. Usually she is glad to see me, and happy to talk. Usually she has nothing to hide.

"So talk," she said.

"Janine! Come on, open up. What is it with you lately?"

"What do you mean?"

"I *mean*, Janine, why are you being so secretive? Why are you hiding behind closed doors? Why are you lying to Mom and Dad? And why are you using my phone without permission?"

Suddenly Janine threw the door open. She was dressed, once again, in my red sweater — and she was wearing plenty of makeup. "And why are *you* giving me the third degree?" she asked. "Can't a person have her own life around here? Why does everything I do have to be everybody else's business?" She stomped past me, down the hall and down the stairs.

"Janine," I called. "Wait! Where are you going?"

"Out!" she yelled. And then I heard the front door slam. Janine was gone. I stood in the hallway, amazed. My plan to confront her had backfired. Obviously, talking things out with Janine was not going to get me anywhere. I thought for about two and a half seconds, and realized what I was going to have to do. I was going to have to tail Janine again

I ran downstairs and out the door. By the time I reached the sidewalk, Janine was nowhere in sight, so I had to guess which way she'd gone. I turned right, figuring she'd gone the same way she went *last* time I followed her. I jogged along, keeping my eyes peeled for that red sweater. There it was! Janine was in front of me, about to take a left off Bradford Court. I ducked behind a bush.

Janine waited until it was safe to cross, then walked quickly across the road. She turned again, onto Rosedale Road, following the route she'd taken the last time. I hurried along, making sure to keep myself hidden. My sister never glanced back, though. She just walked fast, checking her watch once in a while.

"She must be meeting someone again," I said, under my breath. I'd learned a lot from Derek.

When she arrived at the high school, Janine started to look around as if she were trying to find someone. A few kids were hanging out in front of the school, but I didn't see that guy she'd met the other day. Apparently, Janine didn't see the person she was looking for, either. She sat down under a tree and pulled a book out of her shoulder bag.

"Good old Janine," I said to myself. She can't stand to sit around doing nothing. Janine always has a book with her, in case she has a few minutes to fill up. She'd never just sit and watch people go by, or look at the clouds. Not Janine.

Since Janine was so busy reading, *I* saw the guy she was meeting before she did! It was the same gorgeous guy we'd seen the last time. He drove up — that's right *drove* up — in a cool little red car, and parked near the tree where she was sitting. Then he sat and looked at her for a minute, smiling to himself. Maybe he was noticing her book and thinking the same thoughts I had been thinking. Janine didn't glance up, so finally he got out of the car and stepped over to her. He said something — I couldn't hear what — and Janine jumped a little, as if she'd been surprised. Then she stood up and brushed off her skirt. She smiled at the guy and showed him the book she was reading. He took it and looked through it for a second, and I wondered what could be so interesting. But then he just gave it back to her, and she put it away.

They stood and talked for a while, and I started to get bored. So far, I hadn't learned anything.

But then Janine walked over to the little red car and *got into it*! When the guy got in, he started it up, and they drove off. I stepped out from behind the bush where I'd been hiding and stared after them with my mouth hanging open. The little red car putt-putted down Rosedale and then turned right. I couldn't believe my eyes. Janine had just gotten into a car with a stranger — well, he was a stranger to me — and driven off.

I stood there for a little longer, until I realized there was no point in staring down the empty street. Janine was gone, and I couldn't follow her any more that day. I walked home slowly, thinking over what I'd seen.

My parents were home by the time I got there, and I jumped right into helping them make dinner. I was glad to forget about being a detective and just wash lettuce for a while. I didn't bring up the subject of Janine, and neither did they. We talked about baby-sitting, and school, and stuff like that.

I was in the kitchen with my dad when Janine came home a little while later. My mother was in the dining room, and I could hear her talking to Janine.

"Hi, honey," Mom said. "You're just in time to help me set the table. Have you had a nice afternoon?"

"Oh yes," said Janine. "I was working at the college chemistry lab."

CHAPTER 14

I almost dropped the bowl of salad I'd been holding. It was one thing to know Janine had been keeping secrets and telling my parents little fibs once in a while. But it was another to *hear* her lie — right to Mom's face! Now, I'm no goody-goody, and I admit I don't always tell the whole truth and nothing but the truth, but when I heard Janine lie like that, I was shocked.

"How could she — " I started to say.

"What?" asked Dad. He was standing at the sink, peeling carrots.

"Nothing," I said. I put down the salad bowl and picked up the bread basket. "Is this ready to go out on the table?" I asked my dad.

"Sure," he said. "Take the butter, too."

I stepped into the dining room and set the basket and the butter dish down. Janine was walking around the table, putting a folded napkin at each place. She looked up at me. "Hi, Claud," she said, smiling.

"Hi," I said, without smiling back. I gazed into her eyes, and thought I saw a flash of nervousness there. "So have you found a cure for the common cold yet?" I asked. "I heard you were at the lab this afternoon."

"No cure yet," she answered, "but we're still looking." Her tone was light, but I thought I could hear a little tension in her voice. She put down the last napkin. "All done, Mom," she said. "I'm just going to run upstairs and change before we eat, okay?"

"Sure, honey," said Mom. "Take your time. The chicken won't be done for another fifteen minutes."

I watched Mom smooth out the tablecloth and wipe a smudge off one of the glasses. She looked up at me. "Anything wrong?" she asked. "You're awfully quiet all of a sudden."

"I'm okay," I said. I was quiet because I was thinking. Thinking hard. I had realized something. I'd been following Janine around and playing detective just because I was curious about what she was up to. I'd kind of been thinking of myself as the Nancy Drew of Stoneybrook. But this wasn't just some story, made up to entertain people. This was real life. And Janine could be heading for trouble. After all, I'd seen her get into a car with a strange guy. Cute, yes. But not a familiar face. And then she'd lied to Mom about where she'd been.

What if Janine was in some kind of trouble already? What if that guy was a drug dealer, or some other type of criminal? What if he had Janine under his spell? What if he'd threatened to kill her if she told anyone she'd been with him? Maybe *that* was why she'd been lying!

I knew I was getting carried away. It was unlikely that Janine was involved with some evil lawless mastermind. But still, she really could be in trouble. It was then that I realized I should probably tell my parents everything I knew.

I struggled for a moment with the idea. After all, nobody likes a tattletale. My parents have never encouraged Janine and me to report on each other's behavior. Even when we were young they wouldn't listen when we came running with stories about how one of us had knocked over the other one's blocks.

Suddenly I realized my mother was staring at me. I was still standing at the dining room table, gripping the back of my father's chair. I was breathing hard, and I could feel that my cheeks were flushed. "Claud?" Mom said. She put her hand on my forehead. "Are you feeling all right? You don't look well."

"I'm fine, Mom. But — " I paused. "But I

think there's something you and Dad should know."

She looked at me curiously, but instead of asking any more questions, she just took my arm and steered me toward the den. On the way, she called to my dad. "Honey? Would you please come into the den for a minute?"

"Be right there," Dad replied.

A couple of minutes later I was settled in the big chair in the corner of the den. Mom and Dad were sitting opposite me, on the couch. "What is it, Claud?" asked my mother. She looked very concerned. "Is it about your schoolwork?"

"Are you having trouble keeping up?" asked Dad gently. "We're always here to help, you know."

"It's — it's not me," I said. They raised their eyebrows. Usually I hate the fact that I'm always the "bad daughter." But this time I couldn't take any pleasure in the fact that Janine was the one who was misbehaving. I was too worried about her.

"Go on," said Dad. He leaned forward.

"It's Janine," I said. "I don't know exactly what's going on, but I think she could be in trouble."

Mom frowned. "What do you mean?" she asked. "I know she's been late a few times, and she wasn't entirely honest about where she'd been that night, but I think she under-stands now that we expect the truth from her."

"I wouldn't be so sure about that," I muttered.

"Claudia," said my father sternly. "Why don't you just tell us what this is all about?"

"Okay," I said. I took a deep breath. "The thing is, Janine *isn't* being honest with you. You know how she said she was working at the chemistry lab today?"

My parents nodded.

"Well, that's not true," I said. I started to talk fast. "She was here when I got home from baby-sitting this afternoon. And then she left and she met this guy and got into his car with him and drove off." I stopped for a breath.

"What?" both of my parents said at once. Then they started to ask a million questions.

"How do you know this?" asked my father.

"Who was this 'guy'?" asked my mother. "Did you know him?"

"What do you mean she drove off with him?" asked my father.

"Where did they go?" asked my mother.

I held up my hands. "Wait, wait," I said. "I'll start from the beginning."

"All right," said my father. "Go on." He crossed his arms.

I told them everything I knew, and I told them how I'd found it out. I could see that they were unhappy with the idea of my "detective work," but they let that pass for the moment. As soon as I had finished, my father stood up and opened the den door. "Janine!" he called. "Please come down here for a moment. We need to talk."

When Janine walked into the den, I stood up to leave.

"Oh, no," said my mom. "You stay here. This is going to be a family conference. Why don't you tell Janine what you just told us?"

It wasn't easy, but I did it. Janine stared at me angrily the whole time. "How could you?" she hissed, when I'd finished. "You little sneak." Then she turned to my parents. "I think I better clear some things up," she said.

My father nodded. "We'd appreciate that."

"Well," said Janine. She paused for a moment, and seemed to gather herself together. Then she looked straight at my mother and said, "I have — I have a boyfriend."

You wouldn't believe how quiet that room became. My parents looked as if they'd just heard that the sky was actually green and the grass blue. As for me, I was sure I couldn't possibly have heard Janine correctly.

"A what?" I asked.

"A boyfriend," said Janine. "His name is Jerry Michaels. I met him at the college. He's a junior in high school, like me, but he's in advanced placement, too."

My parents were still looking stunned, so I said, "But he's a total hunk!" I said.

Janine nodded, looking miserable. "That's one of the reasons I kept it so quiet," she said. "I've always hated people who put physical appearance first. I never understood girls who wore makeup, or spent money on clothes, just so they could attract cute guys. To me, it's a person's mind that matters."

"But lately you've been wearing makeup and dressing better," I said. "Was that to attract Jerry?"

Janine nodded again. "But I found something out today," she said. "He said he liked me in *spite* of the way I look, not because of it. So I'm going back to the old me. I was never comfortable wearing all that stuff on my face. I just thought it was the only way to get Jerry's attention."

"So he's a hunk *and* a genius," I said. "He sounds perfect for you. What's the problem?"

Janine glared at me. I was so fascinated by her news that I'd almost forgotten she was mad at me. "Maybe the problem is that I'm a very private person," she said stiffly. "I'm not used to other people knowing my business. I guess I wanted to keep Jerry to myself for a little while."

"I can understand that," said my mother softly. She'd finally come out of her state of shock, and she was gazing fondly at Janine. "I felt the same way when I met your father." She reached over and took my dad's hand. He smiled at her. "Janine," she went on, "I'm very happy for you. But I'm also disappointed. I may have wanted to keep your father a secret when I met him, but I never lied to my parents. And I would not have expected you to lie to us."

"That's right," said my father. "You've earned yourself another two days at home. You're grounded — and I hope I'll never have to say those words to you again."

"You won't," whispered Janine, looking down at her hands.

"One other thing," said my father, sounding even more serious. He paused until Janine looked up at him. "When are you going to bring Jerry home, so we can make sure he's good enough for you?" He smiled at her, and she smiled back, a little nervously.

"Yes," said my mother. "I'm looking forward to meeting him."

"You mean I can keep seeing him?" asked Janine.

"Of course," said my mother. "You just have to promise to be honest with us about where you're going, and with whom."

"Oh, I will! We never go anywhere special, anyway. Most of the time we just find a quiet place to study."

I rolled my eyes. It figured. Janine gets a boyfriend, and all they do is *study* together. Most couples go to the movies, or out for dinner. But Janine and Jerry just want to crack the books. They were made for each other.

I thought again about how cute Jerry was. "Does he have a younger brother?" I said, grinning. "Like, maybe an eighth- or ninth-grader?"

Janine didn't grin back. "No," she said shortly. "Just sisters."

I could tell she was going to stay mad at me for a long, long time.

CHAPTER 15

"So that guy is actually Janine's *boyfriend*?" asked Mary Anne. She shook her head in disbelief, and then helped herself to one of the Yodels I was passing around. We'd already covered our club business, so I was using our BSC meeting to fill my friends in on the solution to the big mystery.

"That's right," I said. "His name's Jerry, and he's a genius, just like Janine. How about that?"

"I think it's wonderful," sighed Mallory. "A secret love is so romantic."

"To tell you the truth, I'm sort of disappointed," said Jessi. She was next to Mallory on the floor, but instead of sitting still, she was doing one of her ballet stretches, with her head all the way down on the ground between her legs. She looked up. "I mean, I was really hoping Janine was a kleptomaniac, at the very least. Something *interesting*, you know?"

128

"I agree," said Kristy. She tucked her pencil over her ear, and leaned back in the director's chair. "But still, I'm happy for Janine."

"Me, too," said Dawn. "A boyfriend with a little red car! She's got it made."

Stacey sighed. "I can't believe we all laughed the other day when Mallory guessed the truth. Now it seems so obvious that she was right."

"It does, doesn't it?" I asked. "But, you know, if it had been anybody but Janine, I would probably have guessed right away. I just never thought of her having a boyfriend before. Especially such a cute one." I unwrapped another Yodel. "It just goes to show you — " I started to say, and then the phone rang.

Kristy grabbed it. "Baby-sitters Club," she said. "Kids are our business." She listened for a moment, and then smiled. "That's great, Derek," she said. "You must be relieved." She listened again. "Oh, well. There's always next season." A few moments later she hung up. "Guess what?" she asked us. "Derek's agent called and told him the writers for the show have decided to forget about the kiss. They think Waldo's too young."

I couldn't believe it. "After all that nervousness!" I said. "But Derek must be happy."

"Not really," said Kristy, laughing. "He said

he had just gotten psyched up for it, and now he's disappointed that it's not going to happen!"

Mallory giggled. "I bet my brothers will be disappointed, too. They couldn't wait to see that episode!"

"I was looking forward to it myself," I said. "Oh, well. At least Derek learned something about truth and lies because of this."

"So did Janine," said Stacey. "Only I bet *she* isn't going to put off kissing for another year!"

We started to giggle. I tried to imagine Janine kissing a boy, which only made me giggle more. Pretty soon my friends and I were laughing so hard we couldn't stop, not even when I heard a knock at the door. "Come in!" I finally gasped, and Janine poked her head into the room.

"What's so funny?" she asked.

"N — nothing," I said, trying to catch my breath. "What's up?"

"I just wanted to tell you that I'm going over to Jerry's house to study. And then he's coming here for dinner. Will you *please* try to act like an adult around him?" She frowned at me. "Or is that too much to ask?"

She was still mad at me. "I'll do my best," I said. "I promise not to suck my thumb or spit baby food on him." I wanted to see if she would crack a smile. She didn't. She just frowned even harder and then closed the door and clomped down the stairs. I turned to my friends and shrugged. "Do you think she'll ever forgive me?" I asked.

"Someday," said Stacey. "But you may have to be patient. She seems pretty mad."

"She is," I said. "Stubborn, too. I've apologized all over the place, but she just doesn't seem to hear it." I hated having Janine mad at me, and I was sorry I'd spied on her, but I knew I'd done the right thing when I told my parents. She did, too. She just couldn't admit it.

Our meeting broke up soon after Janine's visit, and I went downstairs to help my mom with dinner. I could tell she was a little nervous about Jerry coming over, because she kept checking to make sure that the tablecloth was clean and that the silverware all matched. Also, she was worried about the food she was planning to serve. "I hope he likes chicken," she said at one point.

"Mom," I said, "everybody likes chicken. Unless they're vegetarians or something."

"Vegetarians!" said my mother. "I didn't even think of that. What if he doesn't eat meat at all?"

"Then he'll have to get by with baked potatoes and salad," I said. "He'll live." I gave her a hug. "It's going to be fine," I said.

"I know," she answered. "It's just that this is the first time one of my babies is serious about somebody. You're both growing up so fast!" She hugged me back.

The table was set and dinner was ready by the time Janine and Jerry walked through the front door. Janine introduced her friend to us, blushing. Dad shook his hand, Mom smiled at him, and me? I just stood there. He really is the most gorgeous guy I've ever seen up close. He looks like he could be on TV.

But he wasn't conceited or anything. In fact, he turned out to be really nice. He ate everything we'd cooked, and he kept saying how good it was. He asked my dad about the stock market (my dad works for an investment firm), and he talked with my mom about funding for the library. Then he turned to me. "Janine tells me that you're the vice-president of a successful business," he said, grinning. "That's really impressive."

"Uh, thanks," I said, blushing. I must have sounded like a jerk. I closed my eyes for a second and tried to pull myself together. I knew I should ask *him* a question, to make him feel comfortable. "Um, what are you studying in school?" I asked finally. I tried to look at him, but it was hard. He was too cute — he made me nervous.

"Well, I'm most interested in physics," he

132

said. "Nuclear physics, actually. You know, like quarks and things like that."

"Quarks," I repeated. I'd never heard of a quark. It sounded like something a weird duck would say. But I smiled at Jerry, and nodded. "That's great," I said. Then I pretended to be very, very interested in my baked potato, so I wouldn't have to say anything else.

My parents asked Jerry about a million questions — where did he live, and how many sisters did he have, and that kind of stuff. He gave polite answers, and I could tell Mom and Dad were impressed with him. Janine sat next to him, smiling. She looked happy, and very proud of him.

Somehow, we made it through that meal. I didn't spill gravy down my shirt, and my father didn't ask any uncomfortable questions, and my mother didn't tell any stories about cute things Janine had done as a baby. In other words, we didn't do anything to embarrass Janine.

After dessert, we said good night to Jerry, and Janine walked him to his car. I started up the stairs, since I had homework to do. Then I heard Janine come back in. She went into the living room where my parents were sitting. I paused on the stairs so I could hear what she said to them. "I just want to thank you," I heard her say. "Jerry really liked you both."

"We liked him, too," said my mother. "He's welcome anytime."

"He's a fine young man," added my father.

I rolled my eyes. Dad sounded like the father on some old TV show!

"Well, thanks again," said Janine.

I wondered if Janine would thank *me*. After all, I had done what she'd asked and acted like an adult. I'd done my best, anyway. But I had a feeling she was still mad at me, since she had hardly spoken to me during dinner. I heard her start up the stairs, so I ran to my room and closed the door. I didn't feel like being glared at any more that day.

I started in on my math homework, but before long I got stuck. I'll never understand why I need to know how to find the lowest common denominator. I'm *positive* I'll never use that in my adult life. I put down my math book and picked up the Nancy Drew I'd been reading. Then, just as I was getting to a really exciting part, I heard a knock on my door. "Come in," I said, expecting my mother.

It was Janine.

"Hi, Claud," she said. "Listen, I just wanted to thank you for being nice to Jerry."

"No prob," I said. "He's pretty nice himself."

"He said he thought you were really sweet — and cute."

134

I blushed. "He's crazy about you," I said. "I could tell by the way he looks at you."

"Really?" asked Janine. "You mean that?" Now she was blushing. "Well, anyway — " She paused for a minute. "I'm sorry I got so mad at you. I know you feel bad about spying on me, and I have to admit that I probably shouldn't have been lying and sneaking around. I just — "

"It's okay, Janine," I said, feeling mature. "Having a boyfriend is new for you. You didn't know how to act."

"That's right," she said. "I didn't. And I sure took some wrong steps along the way."

"That blue eyeshadow, for example," I said, grinning.

Janine looked hurt for a minute, but then she laughed. "Jerry *hated* that!" she said, giggling. I hardly ever hear Janine giggle. It sounded nice.

I sat on the bed and patted the place next to me. "So tell me everything," I said. "Like, why did you shake his hand that first time I followed you? I mean, people don't shake hands with their boyfriends."

"Well," she said shyly, "I guess we just weren't up to the kissing stage — yet." She glanced at me and smiled.

"Yet!" I said, raising my eyebrows. "Does that mean — ?"

She nodded, and I shrieked, "Oh, my lord!" I rolled over onto my back. "Janine, you really do have a boyfriend, don't you?"

"I really do."

We talked for about an hour after that, and she told me a million details about Jerry. I heard about the notes he liked to send her in the mail. (I guess I'd seen one of them get delivered!) I also heard about what his favorite foods and colors are, what kinds of music he likes, and why he doesn't wear wool shirts. (Because wool makes him too itchy, in case you're dying to know.) I even learned what his and Janine's "song" is — it's that one that got stuck in my mind that morning not long ago. No wonder Janine acted so strange when I sang it. Anyway, it was great to talk with Janine again, and *really* great to see how happy she was.

Before she left my room that night, Janine helped me with my math homework. And I gave her my red sweater — for keeps. It was good to be friends with my sister again.

About the Author

ANN M. MARTIN did *a lot* of baby-sitting when she was growing up in Princeton, New Jersey. She is a former editor of books for children, and was graduated from Smith College.

Ms. Martin lives in New York City with her cats, Mouse and Rosie. She likes ice cream and *I Love Lucy*; and she hates to cook.

Ann Martin's Apple Paperbacks include *Yours Turly, Shirley*; *Ten Kids, No Pets*; *With You and Without You*; *Bummer Summer*; and all the other books in the Baby-sitters Club series.

THE BABY-SITTERS CLUB

Look for Mystery #7

DAWN AND THE DISAPPEARING DOGS

After dinner, Mary Anne went upstairs to call Logan. I settled in on the living room couch. Since I knew I didn't have much homework, I decided to relax for a few minutes and read that day's Stoneybrook News.

I glanced at the headlines and checked the weather. Then I started to page through the paper, looking for the funnies. But something on the second page caught my eye.

DOG DISAPPEARANCES PLAGUE TOWNS the headline read. "Wow!" I said. I took a deep breath and began to read the article.

STONEYBROOK. The Stoneybrook police report a sudden increase in the number of missing dogs from homes in Stoneybrook, New Hope, Lawrenceville, and other nearby towns.

"Owners are reporting missing dogs at a rate I've never seen before," said Police Chief John Pierce. "The dogs have been disappearing from yards and from public places, such as parks."

The article went on to say that nobody had actually *seen* their dog disappear, and that investigation had turned up very few clues for the police to follow up. In almost every case, the dog had simply been unclipped from a leash or chain, and there was never any sign of struggle.

I couldn't believe my eyes. This sounded just like what had happened to Cheryl — and to Shannon! My heart was pounding as I continued to read.

"Without any evidence to go on, we have no way of proving this," said Chief Pierce, "but we do believe that these dogs may be being stolen, perhaps by a ring of professional thieves. We will continue to search for clues and to pursue any evidence we turn up. Meanwhile, we are advising pet owners to be alert."

"Stolen!" I said out loud. "Oh, my lord!" This was incredible. Was there really a dog-theft ring operating in Stoneybrook?

Mysteries:

THE BABY-SITTERS CLUB®

by Ann M. Martin

More titles... ➤

The Baby-sitters Club titles continued...

❏ MG43568-X	#39 Poor Mallory!	$3.25
❏ MG44082-9	#40 Claudia and the Middle School Mystery	$3.25
❏ MG43570-1	#41 Mary Anne Versus Logan	$3.25
❏ MG44083-7	#42 Jessi and the Dance School Phantom	$3.25
❏ MG43572-8	#43 Stacey's Emergency	$3.25
❏ MG43573-6	#44 Dawn and the Big Sleepover	$3.25
❏ MG43574-4	#45 Kristy and the Baby Parade	$3.25
❏ MG43569-8	#46 Mary Anne Misses Logan	$3.25
❏ MG44971-0	#47 Mallory on Strike	$3.25
❏ MG43571-X	#48 Jessi's Wish	$3.25
❏ MG44970-2	#49 Claudia and the Genius of Elm Street	$3.25
❏ MG44969-9	#50 Dawn's Big Date	$3.25
❏ MG44968-0	#51 Stacey's Ex-Best Friend	$3.25
❏ MG44966-4	#52 Mary Anne + 2 Many Babies	$3.25
❏ MG44967-2	#53 Kristy for President	$3.25
❏ MG44965-6	#54 Mallory and the Dream Horse	$3.25
❏ MG44964-8	#55 Jessi's Gold Medal	$3.25
❏ MG45575-3	Logan's Story Special Edition Readers' Request	$3.25
❏ MG44240-6	Baby-sitters on Board! Super Special #1	$3.50
❏ MG44239-2	Baby-sitters' Summer Vacation Super Special #2	$3.50
❏ MG43973-1	Baby-sitters' Winter Vacation Super Special #3	$3.50
❏ MG42493-9	Baby-sitters' Island Adventure Super Special #4	$3.50
❏ MG43575-2	California Girls! Super Special #5	$3.50
❏ MG43576-0	New York, New York! Super Special #6	$3.50
❏ MG44963-X	Snowbound Super Special #7	$3.50
❏ MG44962-X	Baby-sitters at Shadow Lake Super Special #8	$3.50

Available wherever you buy books...or use this order form.

Scholastic Inc., P.O. Box 7502, 2931 E. McCarty Street, Jefferson City, MO 65102

Please send me the books I have checked above. I am enclosing $ _____
(please add $2.00 to cover shipping and handling). Send check or money order - no
cash or C.O.D.s please.

Name _____

Address _____

City_____ State/Zip _____

Please allow four to six weeks for delivery. Offer good in the U.S. only. Sorry, mail orders are not
available to residents of Canada. Prices subject to change.

Pssst... Know what? You can find out **everything** there is to know about *The Baby-sitters Club*. Join the BABY-SITTERS FAN CLUB! Get the hot news on the series, the inside scoop on all the Baby-sitters, and lots of baby-sitting fun...just for $4.95!

With your **two-year** membership, you get:

☆ An official membership card!
☆ A colorful banner!
☆ The exclusive Baby-sitters Fan Club quarterly newsletter with baby-sitting tips, activities and more!

Just fill in the coupon below and mail with payment to:
THE BABY-SITTERS FAN CLUB,
Scholastic Inc., P.O. Box 7500, 2931 E. McCarty Street, Jefferson City, MO 65012.

- -

The Baby-sitters Fan Club

❑ **YES!** Enroll me in The Baby-sitters Fan Club! I've enclosed my check or money order (no cash please) for $4.95 made payable to Scholastic Inc.

Name _____ Age _____

Street _____

City _____ State/Zip _____

Where did you buy this *Baby-sitters Club* book?

❑ Bookstore   ❑ Drugstore   ❑ Supermarket   ❑ Book Club
❑ Book Fair   ❑ Other_____(specify)
Not available outside of U.S. and Canada.

BSC791